PRAISE FOR
INTO THE ATTIC

"A novel that offers a multilayered exploration of the afterlife, grief, and moving on . . . Over the course of this novel, Sherman brings the past into contact with the present to illustrate what it means to come to terms with one history and truly let go of the past. Supernatural elements, introduced early on, create a sense of mystery and suspense, while a poignant, deeply emotional tone is established well . . . Sherman's prose style shows appealing moments of wit, and she successfully conveys a key message: 'Everyone has a different version of the past, even if you were in the same room.' An often-haunting story about memory and loss."

— *Kirkus Reviews*

"A beautifully rendered novel of grief and resilience, *Into the Attic* explores the ways in which the present is haunted by the ghosts of the past. With keen intelligence, humor, and vivid imagination, Ellen Sherman brings to life a cast of unforgettable characters in a tale full of surprises, magic, and illumination. A compelling story about what we hold onto and how we let go of those we love, *Into the Attic* will linger in your heart and mind long after you've turned the final page."

—Nancy Gerber, author of *What the Living Remember*

"When three uninvited guests show up for Thanksgiving dinner, long-held secrets are exposed, old wounds are laid bare, and, amidst the chaos, the beauty of family is revealed. Using suspense and dark comedy, *Into the Attic* unpacks all the things we hold onto, then helps us discover what is indeed worth saving. It is a page-turning ride replete with flawed spirits, regret, acceptance, and above all, hope."

—Lisa A. Sturm, author of *Echoed in My Bones*

"Ellen Sherman has imagined a world where an ordinary woman (Caroline Crane: wife, mother, writer, friend), in the midst of cleaning out the attic where she has lovingly stacked and stored decades of her family's treasured memories, is visited by the Past itself, with its own surprising limitations and demands— and one unexpected, heart-wrenching rule. Artfully blending the surreal with everyday life, the author explores the delicate, ever-shifting balance between remembering and forgetting, holding on and letting go."

—Jane Schwartz, author of *Ruffian: Burning from the Start*

"*Into the Attic* is a poignant and lively exploration of how we evaluate—and reevaluate—the chapters in our lives. How memories aren't records but interpretations that dim or sharpen over time. That varying focus is instructive: the freedom to embrace the future comes only when we're no longer captives of the past."

—Tom Hitchcock, author of DROWNING

"In a spirit of love and abundance, two parents and their two young adult children are gathered for Thanksgiving. Family secrets, among the main veins of storytelling, are also on the menu. Sherman's story literalizes wishes we harbor, often prompted by holidays, for the presence of all our loved ones, those young and alive, and those taken too young or by tragic accidents. We wish for their imaginary presence so we might utter words that remained unspoken, gestures withheld, misunderstandings clarified. However, Sherman also dives deep into what those lost loved ones might wish for. What is death for the living? What is death for the dead? What is grief for the living? And what is grief for the dead? The attic, a metaphor for our minds, with all their clutter and memories, is, in this pleasurable fantastical novel, the place where ghosts announce their fervent wish to be included on this precious occasion."

—Frances Bartkowski, author of *An Afterlife*

INTO THE
ATTIC

Ellen Sherman

VIRGINIA BEACH
CAPE CHARLES

Into the Attic

by Ellen Sherman

ISBN 978-1-64663-838-3

A few lines from the following songs appear in this novel:
"It Ain't Necessarily So," from *Porgy and Bess* by George Gershwin, 1935
"Lament" and "No More," from *Into the Woods* by Stephen Sondheim, 1986
"Stormy Weather," by Harold Arlen and Ted Koehler, 1933

Published by

◤ köehlerbooks™

3705 Shore Drive
Virginia Beach, VA 23455
800-435-4811
www.koehlerbooks.com

In loving memory of
Kathy Sherman and Steve Soltoff,
and for all my loved ones,
both here and out there

You can never go home again,
but the truth is you can never leave home,
so it's all right.
—Maya Angelou

What is the self?
It is the sum of everything we remember.
—Milan Kundera

CHAPTER ONE

*Sift through your past
to get a better idea of the present.*
—fortune cookie

Before Caroline saw them, she smelled them, a potpourri of scents from the past. Her mother's sweet-smelling moisturizer, applied lavishly, which Caroline found cloying even though she liked things sweet. Her dad's sweat, which always surprised her for its pleasantness. And Michael's scent, for which there were no adjectives; only he smelled like that, a smell she was crazy about.

She had finally made it to the attic, third-floor burial ground for memories she had avoided for nineteen years, plus hoards of other stuff. At first, she thought the slew of hours she'd spent up there had produced these idiosyncratic smells that she had not inhaled in years, a trick of the mind as she contemplated her missing people.

In the first few months after the accident, she had stuck her nose into their clothing a lot, trying to inhale them back to life. But with time, the smells had dissipated. They now competed with other attic fragrances. When thick enough, dust has a distinct smell—and decaying bugs, fraying brown manuscript pages, snapped rubber bands. Also, the bygone Bantam, Pocket, and Signet Classics of Shakespeare, Twain, Conrad, and the like, purchased for sixty or seventy-five cents eons ago, their yellowed spines now disintegrating and their pages fraying. *Stuff and bother,* someone had said, perhaps Shakespeare or Dickens, and at last she got it. Stuff *was* bother—because what was she going to do with it all?

Hmm. Perhaps the phrase was *stuff and nonsense?*

In March, Caroline had turned fifty-nine. On her birthday four years earlier, she and Philip had agreed to put the house on the market by the spring when she turned sixty. The idea was to consolidate all the crap in their lives while they still had energy, and move to an uncluttered apartment in the city while still young enough to enjoy it.

She had fantasized about painting all the rooms, refinishing the floors, and adding ceiling fans before hauling their possessions into a new space, something she'd never had the luxury to do in past moves. She kept a folder of design touches, like star-and-cross mosaic tiles for the backsplash. Lately, though, Philip had voiced second thoughts about moving to Manhattan, citing studies that claimed you lived longer if you spent time in nature. He remained gung-ho to downsize, but what about a smaller place in the suburbs?

Time was a-wastin'. The physical contents of their lives were spread throughout the attic, comprised of a long, wide room that ran the length of the house, plus two closets. One closet held clothes, suitcases, and vintage skis; the other, bills, tax documents, printer paper, and toner cartridges, enough legal pads for two lifetimes, and numerous copies of her remaindered novels. A disproportionate amount of everything everywhere was hers. Philip had brought little to their marriage and saved even less, whereas she'd kept every high school paper, poem, journal, essay, and novel draft. There was also much from the lives of others, her others: her two living children, and her dead first husband and parents, who had continued to haunt her daydreams all these years.

"Why do you need to scrutinize everything?" Philip had asked. "Let it go. That's the healthy thing to do."

"I can't," she'd said. "I may need these things for deep background."

She was a writer.

He had laughed, but seeing her pained smile, added, "I'm laughing with you, Caroline. You know that."

Granted, it was a cheap form of torture, surrounding herself with the words, photos, artwork, and cherished belongings of others.

"You could just make things up," Philip offered.

He had a point there. And wasn't it all made up anyway? What she wrote was far from accurate. He had seen it firsthand in her essays when she *borrowed* from him over the years. Facts did not dictate an account; rather, they were in service of it. "No one is safe when I write," she had teased when they first met.

But, of course, it wasn't just because she was a writer that she resisted her husband's suggestion to toss everything wholesale. Although she had great difficulty confronting the stuff, it was a comfort—and an honor—to sit quietly in its company.

Because of them, her lost triad.

◉ ◉ ◉

The smells lingered. She was on her knees, her pants grimy with age-old dirt and the wings of decomposing ladybugs and bees. She jumped at the sight of a yellowish-brown clump on the back of her thigh. But it was merely ancient insulation material that had adhered to her.

"Goddamn you guys. You screwed me up big time," she said to the vast emptiness.

As always, she began with her own things, searching through

carton after carton and making piles along the planked floor until she located a deep box less decrepit than many of the others, one of several she had labeled *ongoing*, meaning it was one she had looked in and added to over the years, as opposed to the mausoleum of boxes on the opposite wall, sealed tight and stacked in rows six high. These contained items inherited and ignored for nearly two decades.

"We will not be bringing boxes upon boxes with us," Philip had said.

She dimly recalled their contents, hastily packed during a state of depression and rage. Stages of grief are not experienced consecutively, but all at once, she had learned. Letters, photos, favorite clothes, tchotchkes. Her mom, like her, had been a journal keeper. Caroline hadn't read them because, had things been reversed and she had died, she sure wouldn't want her mom reading hers.

Whereas Philip sort of understood her hoarding, Michael, her first husband, had abhorred excess and clutter. Apart from an array of sports memorabilia, his entire life savings constituted two boxes, and he hadn't even wanted to hold onto this representative collection of his magazine articles, award certificates, track trophies, and childhood photos—including the cutest one of him at three in a bow tie. Ironically, she had packed these items when he was still alive, insisting he keep them for when he grew old. "You may want to show your grandchildren—you never know," she had told him.

All this time she hadn't looked.

"Proof that you can live without them," Philip had said of the grand columns of boxes belonging to the deceased. They were draped with king-size white sheets, which too had yellowed.

"I need to go through them before I can let go, Philip," she'd protested. There was treasure in the boxes, not just burdensome stuff. Her grandfather's autobiography for one, or at least the sixty pages he had handwritten in a creative frenzy while attempting to recover from open-heart surgery at age eighty. He had been a minor inventor, who, like Caroline, slept with a notepad by his bed and scribbled down inspirations in the middle of the night. His words might come in handy one day, along with the scores of letters from all the people who had passed through her life.

"Some people need things more than others," she told Philip. "Some people are more attached. I promise to winnow it down, but I need to do it thoughtfully. I'm trying, really, but back off. Please!"

Some people had suffered much more tragedy.

"I know I'm whining, by the way," she had added.

She was hopeful about the box before her as she rifled through it once again: manuscripts, articles, and folders labeled *More Ideas* and *Brilliant Thoughts*. The specific article that had precipitated today's search—and upheaval—was about her mother, a piece about all the questions you never got to ask the suddenly departed. Her mother had been fifty-nine at the time of the accident, exactly Caroline's age now. Mother and daughter had been in the middle of a big fight when tragedy struck.

Was that why her mom had accompanied her dad and Michael that night, to get away from Caroline, who was fuming? That's what she always believed, although of late she wondered if her mom had simply wanted to get away from her cranky grandkids, one of them very sick at the time. Her mother had a hard time tuning into anyone under twenty, let alone very young children.

The article in question had been published in a *real*—not virtual—magazine back in the day. If she didn't find it, it could not be recovered with an online search like articles nowadays. It had appeared in the Mother's Day issue of a long-defunct New Jersey magazine. Highly unlikely that any of the local libraries had held onto copies that far back. It had fallen into that weird crack between post-microfiche and pre-internet.

The piece about her mom explored not only things she wished she had asked her mother—family history and the like— but also things she wished she'd had the chance to tell her. There were so many things she wished she could tell the three of them.

Reading it again might help her with her new novel. She could just make everything up as Philip advised—but the piece might serve as a springboard, as personal experience often did.

During her past two weeks in the attic, she had also searched, unsuccessfully, for an article she had published about her dad, centering around something he had said to her a few days before he died, a gift of words she had clung to in the darkest times, when the kids were so little, and she not yet old.

◉ ◉ ◉

She felt low. Really low. It had been years since she felt this sad. "Once in a while, you're down, but it always passes," Philip would say. Like Michael before him, he was an optimist. Or was that just men and their propensity to skip the details?

She blew her nose on the shredded tissue in her pocket, stood up straight, and did a few stretches, taking turns balancing on one leg because it's important to work on balance as you age.

Despite hours upon hours in the attic, she had gotten so little done, staring at the piles, wanting to explore them, but holding back. Were they treasure or bother? It put her in a trance. Maybe the problem was she didn't know where to start. Overwhelmed, she spent most of the time restacking, relabeling, or strewing things about. Ultimately, she might pause and consider one or two items randomly.

Downstairs, she relished the idea of reading the old letters, especially from those who had died. But upstairs, she couldn't bring herself to do it. Something stopped her.

It was like standing at the end of a diving board, paralyzed. When all was said and done, maybe she just didn't want to bother. And wasn't the prevailing wisdom that you should try to stay in the present? Sometimes she wished it would all disappear.

At least she had found a use for the missives. After folding them into origami cranes—the only origami figure she had mastered—she had glued them to a wooden wreath she had picked up at a crafts store. She affixed pinecones too, and some of the yellowed paperback pages that had shaken loose. Even broken rubber bands looked arty when craftily placed. This was to be the Thanksgiving centerpiece, with two large candles at its center.

Ah! Her father's tennis sweater, his most prized item of clothing although it had small holes under the arms and the white wool was dingy. It had looked this shabby when he was alive, but he'd worn it anyhow, all the time. How he loved that sweater! It had bands of green and gold at the V-neck and cuffs. Green had been her dad's favorite color, and so it was hers. He loved playing tennis, so that had become her sport.

She spread the sweater out on the floor and took a few photos with her cell phone in preparation for finally throwing it out. Time to let go. But then she put the phone down and hugged the sweater to her face, her tears soaking it. She inhaled deeply. Although it no longer held his smell, its woolly scent was reminiscent. "I loved you so much," she cried. "Why did you leave me so early? Where did you go?"

Caroline blew her nose some more, then picked up a photo she had recently excavated of her dad with both children on his knees. Mark was four and Julie just six months old, but already attempting to cruise on her belly. Although it was a chilly March, he had bundled them up and taken them outside. He was sitting in a deck chair, smiling, so proud, the light reflecting off his sunglasses and his thick, silver, Norman Maileresque hair. She had taken this picture the day before the accident. He was already an awesome grandfather.

◉ ◉ ◉

Before she saw it, she felt its presence, something else she'd been looking for, its edges sticking out of a plastic Macy's bag, a large rectangular box of blue lacquered wood with an elaborate Arabic design. She lifted the lid.

"What are you dissecting today, Professor Crane?" Philip said.

Caroline jumped and the box's heavy lid slammed shut. He was right behind her, but she hadn't heard him ascend the creaky attic steps, nor walk down the wobbly floorboards in his black work socks, no shoes. Had he tiptoed? Was he trying to catch her at something? She craned her neck to look up at her husband, who was always so happy to see her.

"Maybe enough torture for today?" He nodded as if to say, "You know I'm right," but he still managed to smile.

"Downsizing is like dismantling your life," Caroline said. Dismantling lives, really, because she had carted bags of the kids' stuff out of the attic: Tom Chapin and Rafi cassettes, children's videos, and all but a handful of favorite toys. "We don't want it. Knock yourself out," they had said—of everything.

"I've come to offer my assistance as your sous-chef," Philip said. "The plan was to prepare at least three dishes tonight."

Thanksgiving was tomorrow—she had forgotten! And he had come home early to help.

"Oh, right. Thanks, honey, but I need a teensy bit more time up here, then I'll call it quits for the week. Promise." Continuing to gaze at him, she slid the Macy's bag over the decorative box and stood. If Philip had noticed it, he didn't let on. He was respectful that way—or oblivious. He certainly hadn't noticed her physical state. No words for how dirty she was.

He massaged her neck and shoulders, kissed the top of her head, then turned and headed back to the stairs. Once she was sure he was down, she dropped to the floor again, reopening the lid of the beautiful box.

Michael's love letters were written on light blue sheets, trimmed in gold, in a meticulous print, all caps. He had been a pure writer. Whereas her words were the results of tussles, his flowed out of him and he was never at a loss for a fresh angle. Nine years together. A thick stack of blue sheets.

◎ ◎ ◎

A sudden breeze, though the windows are shut tight. Another, stronger, whiff of Michael. Of her mom. Her dad. Of all she has lost. The smells emanate from behind her. Slowly, still clenching a few blue pages, Caroline stands. The lights dim and she knows, is sure, something's behind her, but she is frozen, too scared to look. Her breath quickens and when at last she turns, they are standing against the wall, her mom in the middle with her arms extended in front of the chests of the other two, like a crossing guard. Does she want to hug her daughter first? Or hold the others back?

They are three-dimensional, but they are in black and white.

"Oh my God—," Caroline says, inaudibly.

"Caroline!" the younger man says.

Like a character in a horror movie, she tries to scream, but nothing comes out. She opens her mouth wide, strains to activate her vocal cords, and finally emits a low "Aaagh." The blue sheets fall to the floor when she presses her palms against her eyes and squeezes them tight. She opens them and takes several steps back. "Whaaa—"

It's them. But it can't be. But it's them. She shivers and sweats at the same time as she lunges at them.

They flatten into the wall like collapsed cartons.

"Don't touch us! You can't touch us," her father reprimands, thrusting his hands, palms outright, to signal she must stand back. Caroline retreats a few steps and the three pop out again.

"That's a nifty trick," she says, no longer afraid because she's decided she's dreaming.

"You can't touch us yet, sweetie. Hopefully soon," Michael says. "And by the way, this isn't a dream. This is real," he adds, seeming to read her mind.

His voice is as powerful and cheerful as ever, and she bursts into tears. That's one of the few things she has forgotten—how much she also loved his voice, a melodious baritone. How much she loved him.

"What's going on here?" he asks, gesturing to the mess in the attic.

She can't stop crying. Eventually, she picks up her sweatshirt and wipes her face with it. "What's going on? You're asking me?" she says, her volume finally on.

The threesome laugh.

"Hello, darling," her father says.

It is them. "Why are you all dressed so funny?" she asks because they look odd. Michael sports a short-sleeve madras shirt in fall colors and blue-striped seersucker pants. They are old and faded, but meticulously ironed, which was so like him. Her mom is in a worn, yellow, polka-dot ensemble, lambswool vest, and desert boots Caroline could swear once belonged to her. A hole has been cut out of the right side of the left shoe so that her big toe in a pilled white sweat sock sticks out. Her dad is wearing tuxedo pants and that beloved, ratty tennis sweater she had just been cradling. She whips her head around to see where she had laid the sweater down on a pyramid of notebooks only a few minutes before. Of course, it's no longer there.

"You get to wear the clothes you loved best," her mother explains. "That's one of the cool parts."

It's especially odd that their clothes are in color, but they are not.

"Weren't those *my* shoes?" Caroline asks her mother. "You've ruined them."

"Bunions," her mom says. "They followed me to heaven. The most important thing is to be comfortable, dear."

Caroline understands. She too has problems with her feet and can only wear real shoes on short walks. She owns three pairs of fancy black sneakers to go with dressy outfits, albeit none she has taken a scissor to.

"Well, you look great, Mom." She is fairly certain that she also packed that polka-dot ensemble into one of the cartons after the accident. She examines her mother more closely. "In fact, you've never looked better."

"Yeah, well, I've had a lot of rest—obviously! But I attribute my fitness to my having been such an athlete back in the day."

"An athlete?"

"I was a very good athlete, Caroline. I was always on the go, playing golf, running, canasta."

"Running? You mean, like jogging?"

"And weren't you an Olympic swimmer, Mom?" Michael asks.

Caroline laughs. He always made her laugh.

Bernice snorts. "Go ahead. Poke fun."

"I don't think I ever saw you jogging. I don't think—"

"I loved to run."

"Girls!" her father says.

"Ladies," Michael corrects him. To Caroline: "Don't take the bait. You always do that!"

"I do not. How can you say that?"

He laughs. "Case in point."

"Where we're from, you can assume your favorite weight," Bernice says. "As long as you truly weighed it at some point— not just for a day after a stomach virus, or colonoscopy, or something like that."

"Wow. That's very cool," Caroline says. "And, really, I'm just so happy to see you all in one piece."

"More or less," Norman says.

Now her mother looks her over and Caroline expects her to comment on how much she's aged and the prominent pimple on her chin, and her generally unkempt state. But Bernice simply smiles, inching toward her, and in so doing yanking Michael and her dad forward too, although she can't see how they're attached.

"It's so good to see you, dear," her mother says.

Caroline exhales. "You, too. I'm sorry if I smell or look disheveled."

"Not at all. You look fine."

Who is this woman? She's so nice.

"It's great to see you, Viv," Norman says. "Hey, remember this?" He tugs at his tennis sweater.

"*Viv?* I'm Caroline, Dad. Why'd you call me Viv?"

"Picky, picky," Michael says, giving her a wink. "Hey, remember your dad's old sweater, Caroline?"

"Of course I do. I don't know how he got it again though, or why he—"

"By the way, we love what you've done with the place," Michael says, surveying the wreckage that had once been the attic. He looks incredibly young, and she realizes he's still forty-two, same as when he died. The ghosts haven't aged at all. Whereas she was once two years Michael's junior, she is now seventeen years his senior. He steps forward, and again the other two come along, seemingly attached by an invisible rope or chains. "Seriously, why is this room such a mess, and where on earth did you get all this stuff?"

"Time's passed," she mumbles, taking baby steps toward them. "Years and years. A lot of time, a lot of stuff. Not to mention, a lot is yours." She gestures to her parents. "Apparently, I'm the family archivist."

She is a few feet from them now, and even in their black-and-whiteness, she can see how wiped out they are, their skin virtually transparent. She is relieved that her dad, at least, has more lines around his eyes and mouth than she. Her folks are now her peers, and Michael is a relative youngster.

"Geez, I never realized how much you look like your mother," Michael says.

"Try not to sound horrified when you say that, Michael," Bernice jokes.

"No, really, you guys could be twins. It's uncanny."

"I'm honored," Bernice says.

It is Caroline who is horrified. Not because her mom looks bad at fifty-nine, but because Caroline herself has not aged well. Although maybe she can't judge. She hates photos of herself in real time, but viewing them twenty years later, she usually thinks she looked pretty damn good.

"I've definitely got a bigger tush," Caroline says.

"Don't be hard on yourself, dear."

"It's rather remarkable," her dad says, and Caroline is uncertain whether he is referring to the resemblance or her tush.

"How's Mark?" Michael asks.

"You're as close to his age as you are to mine now," Caroline says.

"That can't be true, Caroline!"

"Well, almost. He's twenty-three. It's been a while, Michael. Do you guys have any sense of time up there? Out there? And, also, if you can travel and see people, why the hell did you wait till now? How come it took you so long? I could have used you sooner. I've struggled so much, especially at first."

"We've wanted to come from the get-go," Bernice says, "but—"

"But there's this waiting protocol," Michael says. "We can't figure it out exactly. But, believe me, it's not for lack of desire, Caroline—ours or yours."

"It's complicated, dear," Bernice says. "And we don't want to waste the precious time we have with you complaining. The point is, we're here now."

Norman looks confused.

"How's Mark doing?" Michael asks again.

His thick hair is still jet black, and he stares at her the way he did when he wanted sex.

"Mark's fine. He's great, in fact, pretty mature. He'll be home tomorrow. But you know that, don't you? Don't you know everything?"

"We don't, actually," Michael says. "We hardly know a thing."

Caroline's parents shake their heads for emphasis.

"I mean, I did learn my mother died. And that my dad is—"

"Michael!" Bernice shoots him a warning look.

"So sad about Isabel," Caroline says.

"You have a little baby, right?" her father asks. "How's our little baby?"

Caroline sighs. "She's okay. I think. Hardly a baby anymore. It's been nineteen years. But a lot to explain about that one. She's a work in progress."

"I wish I could kiss you," Michael says, staring into her eyes and somehow not turned off by the gray in her thinning hair or the extra pounds democratically distributed, the circles around her eyes, the—

Is it possible they only see her as she was then? Is that why her mom hasn't landed any zingers? How great would that be?

Michael jostles the others as he attempts to wriggle loose from the invisible bonds. "I wish I could touch your breasts and—"

"Michael! My parents!"

He shrugs. "Don't worry about them. We have no secrets anymore."

Her parents do look calm and accepting.

"I wish I could—" Michael sighs. "Not yet."

Uh, not ever, Caroline thinks sadly. *That ship has sailed.* "Maybe just a group hug," she says, lunging at them again.

The ghosts vanish.

CHAPTER TWO

Every exit is an entrance to new experiences.
—fortune cookie

When Philip first met Caroline, one of the few ways he could make her laugh was by telling silly jokes. Although he grew up in New England and she in New Jersey, they had learned many of the same jokes as children. Her favorite, which surprised him given the subject matter, was the one about the singing telegram. It was a joke her father loved to tell Caroline and her brother when they were kids.

An old man hears a knock at the door and answers it to find a young stranger standing before him.

"Telegram," the stranger says.

"A telegram, great. Would you sing it to me? I've always wanted a singing telegram."

"Er, uh," says the young man.

"Please!"

"I don't think you want me to sing this," the young man protests.

"No, really, I insist," says the old man.

*"Well, okay." He clears his throat. "Dah-da, dah-da dah
DAAAH: Your sister Rose is dead!"*

Philip chuckled, then frowned. What the hell was Caroline
doing up in the attic other than scattering things around? Her
mood was extremely up and down of late—even more than
usual. Maybe he needed to tell her jokes again. Sometimes her
intensive efforts made her manic; this evening, she seemed
pensive at best. He hoped to lift her spirits when they cooked,
if only he could get her downstairs. They enjoyed cooking
together, especially for the holidays.

Philip loved the holidays, all of them, and he loved his wife.
She was his third wife, which made him sound like a player, but
it was nothing like that. His first wife was a teacher who divorced
him after two years when she realized she was gay and in love
with her principal. His second wife was really a friend whom
he married on the rebound. They parted amicably—as friends
would—after only a year. Caroline, he explained to everyone,
was his first real wife.

He loved the smells of holiday celebrations: the clove-
infused wreaths his wife picked up for him at Christmas, the
deep-fried smells of Hanukkah, the giant cookie cakes she
baked for all of them on Valentine's Day, even the complex
array of Passover scents, kugel mingled with brisket and her
homemade chocolates. But he looked forward to Thanksgiving
most because the kids would be in their old beds again for three
whole nights—although maybe not this year.

This year Julie had told them not to count on seeing her. At
the start of August, she declared she needed a break and asked
them only to communicate via emails, a putative six-month
experiment. They were four months in and, frankly, she'd been
a lousy correspondent. Luckily, unbeknownst to Julie, Caroline
could still access her daughter's checking account; it was a

college account linked to theirs to facilitate money transfers, and it had never been changed even though Julie had dropped out after one year. Caroline could see that she received a paycheck every two weeks from what Mark described as a hipster clothing store, and to some extent Caroline could track her whereabouts, mainly her prodigious visits to Walgreens, where she seemed to purchase items piecemeal, and Starbucks. "As long as she's picked up her morning latte, I'll assume she's okay," Caroline said, and she checked every day.

Thanksgiving had the best food, and over the years his wife had become an awesome cook. She tossed it off to great effort, claiming she wasn't a natural at anything. He disagreed. She wasn't a natural at self-confidence to be sure, but she had a talent for cooking, writing, and raising kids.

He glanced at his watch, nearly six-thirty. They really needed to get going. She had requested his presence at five and he'd walked through the door eleven minutes after. Very close! After checking in with her in the attic, he had changed and walked the dog. Jupiter had acted strange, barking up at the roof as if she heard weird noises coming from the attic, then skulking away as if she'd been wrong.

After that, he had washed the assortment of vegetables she'd left on the counter. Mostly, though, he'd been waiting.

He paced from room to room. It was a lovely house, spacious and spare, only fifteen miles west of Manhattan and a thirty-minute drive non-rush hour. Because of the proximity to the city, the lots in their neighborhood were not large, but the trees were tall, the sidewalks wide, and the homes charming, no two alike. Architecture firms had always been plentiful in the area, and each house was an original, designed by a unique hand from a variety of styles and materials—stone, brick, Tudors, Dutch colonials, Victorians—and with singular features.

He was no longer keen on their plan to move soon. Of

course, if he could convince Caroline to stay in the suburbs, having a smaller mortgage and lower property taxes would be a big help since they'd had setbacks in recent years, one of them devastating when the 2008 recession hit. They'd been heavily invested in tech stocks. Afterwards, he had foolishly reallocated their remaining, modest holdings to bonds, so their portfolio hadn't bounced back like those of others. Two bad calls there, but at least they had managed without the need of a loan to cover Mark's college costs, including flying him back and forth to Indiana, and a deluxe semester in Australia his junior year. That had been paramount to both of them.

Although the house was less than two thousand square feet, he enjoyed being able to take a little walk without going outside, which was facilitated by the downstairs rooms being connected in a circle. It was one of the many improvements he had helped Caroline make after he moved in with her, and over the years when his cash flow was better. She and her first husband had bought the place as a fixer upper, but never done any fixer-upping, which was so like the guy. It was Philip's idea to open a wall at the rear of the kitchen, allowing you to walk counterclockwise from the front door through the living room, to the dining room, to the kitchen, and then through the small den, which was also his study, and to the front hall once more.

Philip completed two more laps. When he entered his study this time, he had to laugh. Off the edge of the top bookshelf hung strips of Scotch Tape. Caroline had removed these from gifts and packages and was bequeathing them to him to reuse. No doubt she had kept some for herself in her study upstairs. While her habits were chaotic, they were nevertheless economic. She used every inch of every sheet of paper, front and back, large or small. She reminded him of the father in *Cheaper by the Dozen*. Philip appreciated her frugality.

He picked up an almond from the rug beside the couch.

Friends marveled at how neat and uncluttered their house was. Downstairs, Caroline and he were minimalists. But it was like *The Picture of Dorian Grey*. All the documents, relics, secrets, and devilry were in the attic. So, who was he to complain about his wife's current purging up there?

Still, he worried about her delving too deeply into the past. That never led to anything good.

She had told him about this man she often saw, standing at the perimeter of the playground in the local park. He was dressed just so, a golf jacket, pressed trousers, an old man's cap on his head, and his hands clasped behind his back. He wore a half-smile, bittersweet. Those watching him as he lingered, watching the kids in the playground—respectfully, at a distance—might question if he was perverse, but Caroline sensed—knew—that he was simply trying to be in this life, to see the joy. He had lost someone and was very sad.

Philip sighed. She often saw this man, Caroline said. So, she was spending a lot of time in the park by the playground too.

His cell phone rang. Jessica, from his office.

"Philip, I'm sorry to disturb you at home, but I just picked up the messages and the New York Disciplinary Committee called, about the audit. They said you should call them as soon as possible. They're waiting for your call."

"The night before Thanksgiving?"

"That's what they said. I'll text you the number. Everything all right?"

"Not from the sound of it."

Philip unloaded the refrigerator: sweet potatoes, butter, asparagus, meat. He put up a large pot of water. They would need it for something. Soup? Several years ago, he had sat his wife down a week before Thanksgiving and devised a chart with precise times for all preparations on her menu, in fifteen-minute increments, the way he billed clients for his time. He had also listed suggestions for tasks to do while waiting for something to bake or simmer. Caroline had looked at the schedule aghast. She might be economical, but organization, and regimentation, unnerved her.

His cell phone beeped.

Though he'd helped her with the prep for years, he was only good at following instructions in the kitchen in real time and had retained little. At work he made plenty of executive decisions, but he was on autopilot at home. Caroline liked to chide him about this every time he backed down the driveway and headed east to their local bar and grill when heading west was, arguably, the more efficient way to go.

"It's just not logical," she complained.

She might have a point, but he had one too: "When you drive, you can take any route you like. I don't tell you how to go." A solid rebuttal, and to her credit, she had stopped remarking about this.

His cell beeped again, prompting him to look. Jessica's text with the phone number for the Disciplinary Committee. He retreated to his study to make the call.

When he hung up, he felt sick. Ted, his partner and the bane of his existence for years, had apparently cleaned out their escrow account.

To be clear, John Peters, the apostolic-sounding man on the phone, hadn't accused Ted. He had simply stated that the firm's escrow account was empty and asked who had access to it. The answer, of course, was Ted and Philip, and only them. It was a very small firm. Money came and went in escrow accounts, which were used to hold deposits and settlement payments. Philip believed Ted had recently put more than a quarter million into it, a good-faith deposit on a mid-town restaurant under contract. "Based on your records, three hundred and sixty thousand and change should be in the account," Mr. Peters had said. In short, Philip was screwed. He had defended a lot of legal malpractice cases over the years, and now he was the one who needed an attorney.

His call to Ted went straight to voicemail. "We need to talk, obviously," he said. "Call me."

He glanced at his watch. *Okay, Caroline—enough already*! As he pulled down the hatch and guided the folding attic steps to the floor for a second time, he marveled that she had pulled them halfway up again after he'd left her earlier. What was with that? Why couldn't the steps stay down until she called it a day— or night—up there, until she returned to her real life once more? The stairs were rickety and steep. The second-floor ceilings were unusually high, which meant more steps than you'd expect. That made them more treacherous, and he worried about her using them so frequently, especially negotiating them after the attic had put her in one of her states.

She was in one of those states now, sitting cross-legged on the floor at the far end of the cavernous, musty, dusty, room, rigidly still and so transfixed that again she didn't hear him until he was upon her. "It's enough, Caroline," he said. "Really. Time's up."

As before, she startled and dropped something, this time that decrepit sweater her father had reputedly adored.

When he kissed the back of her neck, it felt clammy. "Now what? What's wrong?" he asked. "You're sweating, and you look really pale."

She handed him the shoddy sweater. "Can you see this? Does it feel warm to you, like someone's been wearing it?"

"Of course I see it, Caroline." He was having difficulty controlling his tone, so he paused. "What do you mean? It feels perfectly normal. More normal than you."

She started to cry.

"I'm joking, honey. Come on. Don't make yourself so sad

again. I say dump all this junk in one bold stroke. We have our future to attend to . . . and lots of other problems." He bent down to hug her.

"So, 'Pull yourself up by your bootstraps, Caroline!' That's what you're really saying, right?" She wriggled out of his embrace.

"In my defense, I've never said that, not once in all these years. Give me a little credit, please."

"Actually, I feel good, excited. This whole project is energizing me, like I'm finally connecting to my past in a good way, something spiritual I can't explain just now. I know I said I'd take a break, honey, but I think I have to keep the momentum going up here." She faced him. "If I limit it to shorter increments, would that be okay?"

She looked different. She was crying, and smiling, and covered with dust. And very pale. "Caroline, what is it? You're white as a—"

"A ghost?"

He laughed. "I was going to say sheet. Or vanilla ice cream, marshmallows, you name it." He yanked her to her feet. "Whipped cream?"

She was staring at a brick wall.

"All I know is, you need a break. Come with me now. I left a pot boiling on the stove."

He literally had to pull her over to the steps, as if she suddenly weighed three hundred pounds and with her looking back over her shoulder all the while. He stopped and hugged her again, but she was rigid in his arms, a dead weight. "Earth to Caroline," he said, waving his hand in front of her haunted eyes. She laughed then, relaxing a little.

◉ ◉ ◉

He had met her on an exit ramp. She had slammed into him

as they fed into a single ramp sloping off Highway 46 at rush hour. She had hit him hard, although if you asked her, she'd say she merely tapped his bumper. That, of course, was a specious argument because, at the time, they both knew to pull over and assess the damage.

Since the shoulder on the ramp was narrow, they each maneuvered their car as close to the guardrail as possible, parked, and turned on their flashers. They stood between their cars talking while others honked and squeezed by them. Back then, she drove a Subaru Outback and he a Toyota Corolla, both gunmetal gray. One man rolled down his window as he tried to pass. "Having a party?" he asked.

From the moment she stepped out of her car, Philip was blown away by her. First off, she was beautiful, tall, and slim, even with her face all red and her mouth pursed in an *I'm all business* expression. Back then, her auburn hair was shoulder-length with cascading waves. But what struck him most were her eyes: large and green with these irregular-shaped gold flecks in them. He'd never seen eyes like those before.

She kept her eyes locked on him and waved her arms in wide circles as she spoke. "I'm sorry I hit you, but I have to say, you had ample time to get in there, in my opinion. I was sure you were going. You even started to go, didn't you, and then stopped again? Anyone would have gone by then. Anyone would have thought you were going. That's the only reason we collided."

"Yes, counselor. Well put," he said, then seeing her confusion, added, "I'm joking."

"Having a fucking party?" the man in the car called out again, having made little progress.

Since both vehicles were okay to drive, Philip suggested they continue their debate in the strip mall directly to the right of the exit rather than stand there chatting amidst all the gawkers. Even flustered and near tears, she had drawn him in, and he was thinking how to parlay their collision into a date. As she'd waved her hands, he had noticed she wasn't wearing a wedding band. He pointed to the row of stores. "Meet you in front of the Starbucks?"

"I'm a DD gal," she said.

"Dunkin' Donuts? We can go there after if you like."

She smiled, warily.

"I'm lucky," he said when they had reconvened in front of Starbucks. "It was a direct hit, but you only got my bumper. Your front end looks worse unfortunately."

"I could care less," she said. "So, you're not going to report me?"

"You mean the accident? To insurance? My car's fine, so no."

"Great. Thanks!"

"Hey, can I buy you a coffee, even at DD if we must. Or maybe a drink's more in order?" The most captivating thing about her was that she seemed to have no idea how gorgeous she was.

"Oh, thanks, but I've got to get home to my kids."

"And husband?" It just came out.

Her face grew flushed. "I had a husband," she said. "He died. In a car accident."

◉ ◉ ◉

That conversation occurred seventeen years ago, and Phillip knew he had not aged gracefully. His hands and neck looked old, his eyes tired, and he was losing hair at the back of his head, typical male-patterned baldness. There was also a depression on the top of his right shoulder from years of carting his briefcase by the shoulder strap as he walked the twenty blocks back and forth from Penn Station to his office. He looked like a swayback mule, although it wasn't noticeable in a dress shirt.

Caroline was five years his junior and, to his relief, she

was aging too, including wrinkles and a little hair thinning, only hers was in the front and much less noticeable than his, thank goodness. Truthfully, he wouldn't have noticed at all, if she hadn't kept pointing it out; but these changes in each other didn't matter. She was the love of his life and had given him the extraordinary opportunity to be a father, to raise two children when he'd had none of his own.

"So, what are we planning with this big pot of water, honey?" Caroline asked, testing him in the kitchen now.

"I've been waiting for you to tell me. But you can't have too many big pots of boiling water, right?"

She laughed, although she still looked ashen. He had added more water to the simmering pot while she'd showered and changed. She always looked pretty when he came home from work, even when she'd been busy herself, writing and running around with the kids.

He settled into peeling and cubing the potatoes and squash. For years, Julie had done the lion's share of assisting as Caroline pulled the Thanksgiving meal together. She had been an avid sous-chef who especially loved baking. But at fifteen, she declared herself a vegetarian, renounced sugar, and never looked back. Even now, when they weren't at all sure she'd show up, they were making extra vegetable courses, including that chickpea and vegetable curry Philip dreaded because a zillion ingredients had to be diced just to yield a large, mushy mound.

Ted wasn't going to call, but how would Philip explain the missing escrow funds to Caroline if he did? Ted and he went back thirty years. They had both been disenchanted with the midsize law firm they worked at, which had two greedy founding partners who showed no signs of changing even as the other partners brought in more and more work. Over time, the undercompensated partners peeled off to join other firms and Philip was invited to go with them, but he had hesitated. Then, ten years ago, he founded his own small firm with Ted, his associate Daniel, now his junior partner, and his paralegal Jessica, who had grown into an able office manager. That was it, the four of them, and for years it worked great because Ted and he had totally separate books of business but supported each other well.

Until last year when Ted announced that what he really wanted was to become a minister. He enrolled at New York Seminary and began working at home on Tuesday and Thursday mornings and attending classes those afternoons. Then he started *working* at home other days too, and his caseload began to diminish. In the last few months, he had struggled to cover his part of the overhead and was wearing Philip down with tiresome arguments that Philip should pay the firm's rent entirely.

"There's no reason I should pay overhead anymore since you and Dan are the only ones using the office," Ted had said.

"But that isn't our deal, that you would stop working. We're partners."

"Too bad. You should understand."

"It's not my fault you've dropped off a cliff. You co-signed the lease," Philip had countered.

"I'm called to a higher vocation."

Ted didn't even know what denomination he wanted to be. *Asinine*, Philip thought.

With the mushroom soup simmering, and the sweet potatoes, squash casserole, and brisket in the oven, they sat down to a sushi dinner Caroline had picked up.

"I'm uncovering some fascinating stuff up there, things I thought I'd lost forever," she said. "I'll tell you more about it soon, I'm too exhausted now. But it's good. I'm feeling better. What's going on with that guy whose partner was screwing him over? Fitzgerald?"

"Still a mess. Turns out his partner was completely

incompetent. He's being investigated by the Bar for letting certain statutes of limitation run out. He basically went AWOL and screwed a lot of their clients. And he certainly wasn't covering his office expenses."

"Unimaginable," Caroline said.

"Happens more than you think. And with small firms, it's the responsible partner who gets screwed. It's not Fitzgerald's fault. His partner was out of control," Philip said.

Funny that she picked this moment to ask about poor Fitzgerald. *Should I tell her about Ted?* he wondered, looking down at his black socks, which were covered with dust from the attic. He wanted to tell her, but it would ruin the holiday and he wasn't—

"Philip, you wouldn't believe what happened today."

He shook off the idea and looked up at his wife. "I'm sorry. What were you saying? What happened?"

Her expression was kind, but impenetrable. "Oh, nothing. It can wait."

They finished their meal in silence.

"Thanks for helping, Philip," she said. "I'm going to make the cobbler now, then call it quits for today. I don't need you if you'd rather watch a game. We're in great shape."

"You sure?"

She nodded.

He turned the TV on loud in the den, then proceeded to the living room to try Ted again. This time it rang and rang. *Bastard!*

He was tired and suddenly found himself worrying about Julie, both that she wouldn't show up tomorrow, and also that she might. Caroline hadn't said anything, but he knew she was worried too. Their daughter would be okay eventually, but she seemed confused the last time they saw her, unable or unwilling to explain her self-imposed exile.

Philip didn't stay long with the Knicks, who had amassed a twenty-point deficit in the fourth, instead turning to the Devils versus the Canucks. Their son, Mark, had played varsity hockey in high school and intramural in college, and over the years that was the sport Philip had grown to appreciate most because everyone moved so fast and at the same time made ridiculously accurate passes, on ice moreover.

When the game was over, the smell of baking apple cobbler drew him back to the kitchen, now cleaned up and Carolineless. He rushed up the stairs to see that—big surprise—the attic steps were halfway down. "Caroline!" he yelled.

"Coming!" she called back. "Give me a sec."

It took a bit for her to appear, and as she descended her expression showed that she was irritated by the interruption, but at the same time sought his patience.

"I needed something, that's all."

"What?"

"Oh, this thing I've been looking for."

"What?"

It took her a long moment to answer. "I couldn't find them," she said under her breath.

"What?"

She just shook her head.

Their plan to move had been built on a dream to spend their retirement years in Manhattan, which wasn't really feasible even before Ted had created this fiasco, and was impossible now. Of late, Philip had tried to suggest to Caroline that she needn't rush so much with the attic consolidation. "It's a great house. We're comfortable here," he told her. "We can stay longer. It might even be prudent."

In addition to his faulty forays with the market, he'd made a bad call by taking on a big contingency case that hadn't yielded much despite years of effort invested, as well as a sizable loan to continue working on it. He had been vague about this with Caroline, so she didn't fully comprehend the implications.

At sixty-four, he didn't need all the headaches coming his way. He was slowing down. While he still worked long days, he now took two-hour lunch breaks to read articles in *The Atlantic* and *The New Yorker* and listen to various podcasts Mark recommended—literary, political, neurological, you name it. Mark, his renaissance son.

Caroline knew that Ted had turned all his attention to religion. Now Philip had to tell her that his partner had absconded with the escrow, and possibly the cash in the operating account, not that the latter had a robust balance.

◉ ◉ ◉

In bed, she let him hold her longer than usual. They used to fall asleep in each other's arms—it was his favorite part of the day, this snuggling—but in the last few years Caroline heated up with prolonged holding, her body like a furnace causing her to break into a sweat. It was incredible how hot she got at night, and how quickly. She reminded him of Firestar, the heroine in the *X-Men* films he used to watch over and over with the kids. He also had to be careful where he placed his arm, not heavily across her chest because that exacerbated her reflux.

"Watch the esophagus!" she would say.

In recent years, she slept with a full-size pillow between her knees to prevent a sore back, and he liked to drape his leg over the end of the pillow, tugging on it ever so slightly, creating a tiny bit of tension. He wasn't trying to drive her crazy. He just liked to see how long before she noticed.

She also was itchy. Spectacularly itchy. World class.

But not tonight. Tonight, after all the activity, she lay very still, eerily still, comfortable and at peace as he caressed her shoulders. This is what came from traipsing up and down the attic stairs. How would he tell her about the news from his office? And when? "I love you," he whispered.

"I love you too," she said in a slow, sleepy voice. "Oh, and honey, that water's still dripping under the sink in the powder room—you know, from the pipe? I'm worried we're gonna get those little field mice and they'll get into things."

"They don't really get into things. They just wander around on the floor."

"They might get into the cereal. Or maybe my papers?"

"Right, because they're big consumers of paper . . . especially fiction, I'm told."

Caroline giggled. "Especially contemporary fiction."

"They have book clubs." He laughed too, surprising himself. She always said he was good at compartmentalizing.

◉ ◎ ◎

At one in the morning, he was thinking that he should have read the signs with Ted, who was flighty, frequently in therapy with his wife, and estranged from his mother and two brothers. Before embracing theology, Ted had spent way too much time brewing godawful beer in his basement, which he prevailed on Philip to sample.

But Philip hadn't sized him up as wantonly unreliable—or criminal.

He stroked Caroline's back to get her to turn over.

"Everything all right?" she mumbled.

"You were snoring like crazy."

"I was? Well, I have a lot to process."

Later, when he got up to use the bathroom, the bed was empty, and he figured Caroline had beat him to it. They often passed each other on such pilgrimages in the middle of the night; "shuttle diplomacy," he called it. But she wasn't in the bathroom and once more the attic stairs were down. This time, she had left a note for him at the base of those unstable steps. *Can't sleep. Don't worry about me. Sorting things out. Just need a little more time up there tonight—alone.*

On her night table, he noticed a sheet of unfamiliar light-blue stationery with gold rimming. Eight words in a large, unfamiliar scroll, block print: *Take care of your dishes. We'll be back.*

Even with one eye closed, that didn't make any sense.

CHAPTER THREE

Let your heart speak to others' hearts.
—fortune cookie

The ghosts are fighting and Bernice is crying.

"Oh, what do you have to cry about?" Norman asks.

"It's ironic, that's all. She says she has lots to tell us, but she has no idea what we've come to hit her with. Our deep dark secret will be crushing, believe you me," Bernice says.

"Don't you think you're being a bit dramatic?" Norman says. "I'm thinking of running for Congress, you know."

"What? What in God's name is he talking about?" Bernice asks, appealing to Michael.

"You're a dramaturg," Norman says.

"No I'm not!"

"I believe the expression is drama queen," Michael says. "Bernice is definitely a drama queen. I know what *my* secret is, but I don't believe I know yours. Do I, guys?"

"You'll learn when your wife does," Bernice says.

Michael rolls his eyes. "Nice. She's not really my wife anymore, you know."

"Yes she is!" the couple says at once.

"No, not technically. Anyway, I have to break my secret too. Poor Caroline. I'm dreading that."

"What's *your* secret?" Bernice and Norman ask.

"Oh, for God's sake, think about it. Hint. You were with me. You have to keep using those old noggins, guys. Use it or lose it."

"My brain's in pig Latin," Norman says.

Bernice nuzzles her nose into his neck. "It's okay, dear."

Tied together by an invisible something, the ghosts take seats on three bridge chairs they've lined up in front of a row of Caroline's piles, and Bernice and Norman immediately fall asleep, holding hands.

Michael sighs and reclines as much as possible given the constraints of being shackled to his in-laws. He needs to tell Caroline his secret soon because he knows she'll figure it out and trip him up.

While this revelation will anger her, he is pleased to have another secret that is sure to delight her, and this one is his alone. Through the attic skylight, he sees a full, orange moon; it is enormous, and it occurs to him that he hasn't seen a moon in nineteen years, or registered day from night, or thought about minutes and hours for even a second.

He laughs at his own joke. *What time is it?* Nineteen years since he'd contemplated the specifics of a moment. Nineteen years. The only thing he knows, it's getting late, and their time here may be running out.

When Caroline and he toured this house before stealing it at an estate sale so many moons ago, they thought it a waste to have a giant skylight in the attic. How much time could anyone spend up there? He scans the piles, both neat and strewn, mountains of boxes, and heaps of everything else imaginable. A lot if your name is Caroline.

In addition to the personalia, she has kept their desks, lined up on a far wall. Norman's large banker's desk with two big file drawers built in, Bernice's ladylike Louis XIV desk, and his own small writing desk. It looks like a desk museum for The Three Bears.

Caroline appears from below, talking. "Where'd you go? You just got here, and you disappear. I need you to stay put. I want you to meet Philip."

Michael stands and for the first time manages to separate himself from her folks by yanking his arms this way and that, contorting his body as if he were in a straitjacket, even though Caroline still can't see how they are tethered. Despite all the jostling, Bernice and Norman's eyes remain closed.

"We will be coming and going. We can't hang around indefinitely," Michael says.

"Why not?" Caroline asks.

"I honestly don't know. We can't stay anywhere too long. For some reason we just can't. But I told you we'd be back. In my note. You didn't see it?"

"I did. Thank you."

"I wanted to give you some space. I know how uptight you get when you're hosting."

"Everyone's a critic. I'm anxious for you to meet Philip, that's all. It's hard to keep sneaking up here. Plus, I know you'll like him. He's very down to earth."

"He's just my Phil," Bernice softly sings, her eyes still shut.

Michael is pouting. "Not yet. We can't meet him yet. I'm working on permission to meet Mark first—he's my top priority, understandably. You get that?"

Norman snores.

"Seems like you're avoiding meeting Philip," Caroline says.

"It's the rules. There are rules where we come from, Caroline. Tons of them."

"You're pissed about him, aren't you? But you must know how hard it was for me all those years. You saw how hard and long I grieved for you . . . for all of you. I was sure you'd understand my moving on, although I never forgot you, or let go of you completely. I mean, I kept all your stuff, right? Look"—she waves her hands in the general direction of the columns of sacred, untouched boxes—"it's yours. And theirs."

Michael wears his tight-lipped, noncommittal smile. "I know, I know. I mean, I know now that you've continued to think about me, but I didn't know before. We basically learn everything once we're here. We ascertain little where we come from, both about the place we've left and where we are in the present. In truth, there isn't much of a present for us yet, although that's supposed to change eventually. That's another reason we've been so eager to visit." He sighs. "It's too hard to explain. But I can see how unhinged you've been, and I'm really, really, sorry, sweetie. Having said that, I didn't know squat about Philip."

"Unhinged is a little harsh. But I was only forty when you died. Did you expect—"

"You weren't even forty."

"Very, very nearly, and what the hell does—"

"Let me talk!" Michael says.

"You're the one who's interrupting! You keep interrupting me."

"Because I'm trying to tell you something, sweetie. I didn't know squat about Philip, but I was going to say I understand. I guess." He knows he sounds so sad. "I get it. I do. But you waited several years at least, right?"

"To remarry?"

"To start dating?"

"I waited some. I kind of skipped the dating phase. I mean, everyone was trying to fix me up, but I wasn't ready, couldn't even think about it, couldn't imagine being ready for years. I had no interest in dating at all. I certainly wasn't looking. But I was a mess, Michael, and while I never thought I could be with anyone else, it just kind of happened. It was another car accident—literally. I hit Philip's bumper, and it was like I got hit in the head, smack. Just something about him."

Michael winces.

"I'm sorry. It must be really hard to hear, but aren't you glad for me?"

"How long ago was this? I mean, how long after . . . you know?" he asks.

"After you died? How many years?" She scrunches her nose. "Two. Almost. The thing is, you'll like him, sweetie. I'm positive."

He softens at her using their endearment, brightens. "You always were a tailgater. Right? I used to beg you to keep a safer distance."

"You're lecturing me about driving safely?" He had a habit of not wearing his seatbelt, which was true the night of the accident. And apparently Bernice wasn't wearing hers either, probably because she was trying to be cool, like Michael. The only cool one, in earnest, was her dad, who was securely buckled in the back seat.

"Still insist on walking between parked cars?" Michael asks.

"You really don't know anything? You haven't been watching us from above? I never believed in heaven, but if in fact it exists, how come you're so clueless?"

"Forget all the movies you've seen, or books you've read. It's nothing like that. We don't know crap, I'm telling you. It's not at all what everyone's expecting. It's confusing, inconsistent, and very mysterious, even when you're within it."

"Ineffable."

He nods. "Precisely."

"Well, my tailgating ended up being a good thing this one time," she says. She hesitates, not wanting to kick a guy when he's down, especially a guy who's dead—the ultimate insult to injury.

She's reminded of an incident that took place years ago,

shortly before he died. She was on the giant desktop computer in their bedroom when Michael came up behind her to ask something. She had been going through her emails, rapidly deleting the junk. At the time, absurdly, she'd been getting a lot of solicitations from swingers; their groups had infiltrated her inbox. She continued deleting these with Michael looking over her shoulder until he abruptly stormed off.

When she found him downstairs moments later, he was furious. "Are you having an affair?" he asked.

"What? Absolutely not. You know I would never do that."

"Well, I saw something from a Harold—"

"Harold?"

"Something about sex, a tryst?"

Caroline laughed. "That's the crazy junk mail I get. I have no idea how they got my email. Actually, maybe you can help me get rid of it."

"I saw something."

"Michael, come look for yourself. Believe me, I don't know anyone named Harold. I don't even register the names I delete because it's spam. Come upstairs with me. Come on. I'm happy to show you."

"Are you being straight with me?"

"Oh, my God, get off it already! If I was emailing a lover, do you think I would calmly continue while you read over my shoulder?"

He was unconvinced.

"You're being ridiculous, you know that. And you could at least give me the courtesy of checking it out. You're welcome to look at everything I've deleted. Please . . . go through my trash."

"No thanks, though it's a lovely invitation. Listen, I need to tell you something. Listen to me carefully," he said, his voice cold and harsh. "If you ever cheat on me, I'll kill you."

Caroline's face heated up. "Thanks. But fine with me. Fair

enough. First off, I never would, but ditto for you, okay? If you cheat, I get to kill you."

◉ ◉ ◉

"What made you think of that?" Michael ghost asks in the attic now.

"Think of what?"

"Those salacious emails you kept getting."

Her heart skips a beat. "You can read my mind?"

His diaphanous hand reaches out to her, but she snaps her hands behind her back. "I thought we're not allowed to touch," she says.

"By now I thought I could try."

"Well, I'll tell you one thing. I don't want you in my head. Please get out!" she says.

"You're the one who fell for someone else."

"Oh, for God's sake," she says.

"Don't take the Lord's name in vain."

"I wasn't looking for anyone, but it was a gift what happened with Philip. For all of us. He and you are very different, which helped." She laughs. "I mean, talk about apples and oranges, and that made it easier because there was no way I was going to replace you. I wanted to hang on to you. I have hung on, you know." She sighs. "It's so frustrating that you don't know any of this."

Michael still looks sad. "I'm telling you, we learn about things selectively and super slowly. Everything's so slow in the afterlife, and there's a dearth of info. Crazy, right? Remember how into the news I was? Up there, they keep us totally out of the loop."

"Who?"

He waves his finger at her. "No, no, no. Can't tell you. Against the rules."

"Ugh. Stop saying that."

Caroline's mother coughs.

"What's with them, anyhow? They're sleeping so heavily."

"They're old and tired, Caroline. They sleep a lot now. Not to mention, it's the middle of the night."

Caroline yawns. "They're my age," she says.

"Not really. They look your age, but inside they're nineteen years older than they were, so much older than you. Your mom's in her late seventies now and your dad's more than that. We still age in our realm, at the same pace as you earthlings. Our outward appearance may not change, but we too are experiencing the long decline to decrepitude. We feel the passing days and years, believe me, even if we don't live them. Which kind of sucks." He bangs the wall. "So, anyway, rest assured, I'm as tired as you. Not to mention, we did a lot of traveling to get here."

"Which you're not allowed to describe, right? Well, you sure don't look older, not even a little. And it doesn't make sense, because if what you say is true, some ghosts would be three hundred or thousands of years old inside. How can that be?"

"At a certain point you become something else."

"Such as?"

He shrugs. "I really don't know how it works. We haven't gotten there yet. We learn on an as-needed basis. I just know that, at a certain point, everything changes. And your folks might be getting pretty close to that point, I'm not sure. As I said, you find things out very slowly where I come from. I've hardly figured out anything yet. I didn't realize so much time had passed."

"So much," Caroline says.

"Let's change the subject. I want to ask you about these photos."

"What photos? Have you been rummaging?"

It's a dumb question because, now that she takes a good

look, it is evident he has sifted through many of the boxes she has kept sealed for years, and also some that belong to her and the kids.

"Hey, stop messing with everything."

"Why? You just said it was ours. And we're on a fact-finding mission."

"Huh?"

"Catching up on what we missed."

"That's not in the boxes," she says.

"Well, I'm going to keep rummaging, boss. You'll at least grant me that, Caroline. Besides, it's impossible to make a bigger mess than you already have. And maybe you've forgotten that they're my kids too? You and they are what's left of my life. The dead live on in the minds of the living, 'their memories are a blessing'—isn't that what they always say in shul? Well, you should know that you and the kids live on in our minds too, even while you've pursued a whole new life."

Okay, lots to unpack here, as the anchors on the nightly news program are fond of saying. She hasn't heard the word shul in years, not since she relinquished their synagogue membership after Julie's bat mitzvah. She and Michael had both been raised in Reform Judaism, but he had been more dutiful, more believing, whereas she was a hardcore agnostic. She had wanted the kids to have a Jewish education out of respect for their father, but she and Philip, a lapsed Catholic, are not big on religion.

Michael smiles. "I'm not very religious either. Not really." He tries a nicer tack. "It's rather adorable how many of your papers have coffee stains on them. Same old Caroline. But these photos are fantastic, and I have lots of questions. Let's start with these two."

While possibly she had perceived that Michael held something in his hand, she only now sees that it's a bunch of photo envelopes. Which is the funny thing about her; she hears everything but observes little. How often had she and Philip left a restaurant, doctor's office, friend's house, anywhere, and he asked, "Could you believe that guy's outfit?" or "Did you notice that crazy painting?" or "Did you see those twenty-five guys in full combat gear with Uzis?" Yet, she saw nothing.

The envelopes Michael holds were processed at ShopRite back in the day when you used a camera and couldn't send the photos on your phone to pharmacies online to print.

"Caroline," Michael interrupts her thoughts. He dangles two photos in front of her.

"Oh, I love these," she says. "They're from a birthday party the Newmans had for their son Adam. Remember little Adam? He's in med school now. Anyway, the kids made these clown pictures at the party, using stickers."

Michael laughs. "Different takes for sure."

In an immaculate, blue-checked collared shirt that he had insisted on buttoning to the top, Mark looks self-satisfied as he holds up his clown, who has a concerned expression, but lots of details: rosy cheeks, eyebrows, a bow tie. There is a large sun sticker in the upper right of the page. In contrast, Julie's white T-shirt is smeared with ketchup, and her clown has a nose on his hat, and two different noses where eyes should be, and another nose for a mouth. She looks unsure of herself, but hopeful as she holds up her work.

"She really likes noses," Michael says.

"Apparently. I mean, Mark is maybe seven and Julie only three here, so you can attribute a lot to that, although I'd say Julie still colors outside the lines while Mark mostly stays in them. Not entirely, though. Remember how people used to tell us how lucky we were because he was so polite, so good—that he never went through the terrible twos? Well, he finally did. At fourteen! He really gave us a run for our money then."

"How do you mean?"

"Oh, let's see. He started smoking pot. He skipped a lot of school. He broke his nose fighting a kid on the Forest Avenue basketball courts. See what you missed?"

"Mark? I can't believe it, but good for him, I guess."

"Good?"

"A kid has to rebel sometime."

"Easy for you to say. You missed it. His grades went down. I got calls he wasn't handing stuff in. We had to monitor his comings and goings. He was lying to us, and he was only in ninth grade. I used to talk to you back then, tell you what was going on."

Michael smiles. "I thought maybe I heard you sometimes. Not the details—transmission is rather staticky where we come from. But I knew you were anguished. And I sensed when things got better too. How about Julie? What's she all about?"

"She's still in her terrible twos!" Caroline's eyes fill. "I think it's my fault."

"Why?"

"I wasn't a picnic to be around when they were young."

She notices something. As they are talking, Michael is acquiring tinges of color, if faint, like she imagines early television. Her parents, still fast asleep in their chairs, remain in black and white.

"Caroline!" Philip called from the land of the living.

Caroline yawns so widely that her jaw catches. "Ow," she says, and as she eases her mouth closed, it emits a tearing sound that hurts.

"I can't believe you still do that thing when you yawn," Michael says. "It's so weird."

When her jaw doesn't catch, Caroline likes to yawn, the wider and longer the better. She once read that the bigger the yawn, the more brain functioning was restored, although she's exhausted just now and not thinking well. Still, it's nice to know her brain believes she has a lot of function to restore.

In his sleep, Norman yawns too, but it is a short, little yawn, as if to prove the point. *Why doesn't Michael need to sleep*, she wonders, although he was always a borderline insomniac.

Philip called out again and Jupiter barked.

"Let me get him—please. You can say a quick hi. You'll like him, I know it."

"Caroline, let it go already. We're not allowed!" Michael says. "We may only be here for you, I'm not sure. I'm working on it, but you have to be patient. It was one of the things I went to find out while you were making your dishes before. I'm still waiting for an answer."

"From whom? Whom did you ask?"

"I can't say whom. Oh, and we may only be able to visit late at night like this going forward. Lots and lots of rules. Your mom likens it to Singapore. But you must trust me."

He's always told her to trust him. She always has.

"Caroline!"

"Coming, honey," she calls to Philip.

"It's all right, girl," she hears him say to the whining Jupiter.

"You call him *honey?*" Michael asks.

"I do, Michael—just like I call you *sweetie.*"

Reluctantly, Caroline allows him to take her hand.

"You'll always be my sweetie," he says. His hand is white and slippery. "Listen, no one can know about us. Really. Not yet. Promise?" He gives her fingers a tight squeeze. "Slimy, right?"

"Like Jell-O." His hand is not only slimy, but cold as stone, like they always say about the dead. Still, she holds on and tries not to show her discomfort.

"I'm coming," she shouts toward the attic opening. "Hey, see if you can ask the rules committee to let you guys downstairs," she says to Michael. "It's Thanksgiving and I'm making a great meal."

Michael lights up in full color. "I love Thanksgiving. But, yeah, that's not gonna happen," he says.

"Honey?"

Philip on the attic stairs!

"I've gotta go, sweetie," Caroline whispers. She relinquishes her first husband's hand and runs over to the stairs yelling, "Coming down, honey!" in the direction of her other husband's voice.

CHAPTER FOUR

He who never looks down falls into a pit.
—fortune cookie

No one could have predicted how slick the roads would be that cold, sleeting evening in March.

"That was a doozy," said an eyewitness.

It was a dark and stormy night.

Tell your doctor if you've been to a place where fungal infections are common.

The accident occurred two days before Caroline's fortieth birthday and was the worst night of her life by a zillion miles. She had thought about writing it up many times, but never could. The accident occurred less than twenty-four hours before what was to be a surprise party for her at a Japanese restaurant. Michael had rented a private room and invited thirty guests, including her parents who had flown up from Asheville. Her folks had announced their intention to move to Asheville when Caroline was thirty-five, two weeks after she announced she was pregnant for the first time. It wasn't lost on Caroline that the first announcement had triggered the other. And that her mother was the instigator.

The party was cancelled, sparing her the task of alerting her friends and remaining family—cousins, two aunts—of the tragedy. Once she let her best friend know, Jean had disclosed the party plans to Caroline, found the guest list on Michael's computer, and made the calls. Caroline suspected it became like "Whisper Down the Lane" after that, with all kinds of speculation about how the car had crashed into a highway median and flipped over, whether Michael had been drinking, and why they were on the Garden State Parkway in the first place when usually one would take local roads to the nearby CVS. Mercifully, what everyone got right was that, instead of a birthday celebration, they would be attending a funeral or paying a shiva call.

They ended up needing two funerals, a joint one for Michael and Caroline's mom, who died instantly, and another for her father, who had been in the back seat and persisted for ten days, mostly in an induced coma.

Michael's parents had stepped up, staying with the kids so Caroline could make lengthy visits to the hospital. Her dad was in a private room, hooked up to a respirator and tubes. At first, he could talk, though in tiny increments. He was woozy from the painkillers and seemed to think he had checked into an avant-garde hotel. "Nice bright room," he had slurred. "I love all the stainless steel." But soon, the pain in his head was too hard to manage, so they put him under.

Caroline sat with her dad in silence for hours. It was more tolerable when the room grew dark, sitting beside him in near blackness, her eyes on the expansive nothingness out the window. She begged him to stay with her. "Don't leave me, Dad, please," she said. "You can't go too. I need somebody to stay with me."

A few times, she brought a boom box with showtune cassettes to play at his bedside: *Oklahoma, The Pajama Game, Take Me Along, Stop the World, I Want to Get Off.* With the music playing, her dad's breathing slowed and grew more peaceful.

"I am one of those people who can't live without her father," she had written in her journal as a child. He had bolstered her confidence, mentoring her on the macro and micro level: *Set your aims high. Always tackle the hardest tasks first. Don't let anyone see you put something valuable in the trunk if you're leaving your car on the street.*

How many times had she pulled over on an isolated street to put something she had just purchased in the car trunk before driving on to meet up with a friend?

Her father wrote her notes of encouragement, mostly about seizing opportunities.

"I've saved every letter ever written to me," Caroline once told Philip.

"That's insane," he had said.

In one dreadful lapse of judgment during that grave period after the accident, she brought the talkative Mark with her to the hospital, and she thought her dad's lips briefly curled into a smile when he heard his small grandson's high, animated voice.

"Where's the real Norpa?" Mark asked, unable to look at the man with the tubes.

Caroline whisked him out of the room. "Hmm, that's strange. I thought Norpa was in that room, but I was mistaken."

"Why you mistaken?" Mark asked and then he used the word *mistaken* three more times that day.

Eventually, Caroline and her brother, Bobby, decided they had to take their father off the respirator, and for a short time, he drifted in and out. They never told him of his wife and son-in-law's fate. He'd had to learn that in heaven!

Moments before he died, Norman opened his eyes wide.

"I love you, Dad," Caroline said. She still had the key to her childhood home on her keychain.

"Thanks for sitting in the chair," he said. His last words.

◉ ◉ ◉

The night of the accident, Jean was the first one Caroline called after getting the news. That came via the police after she'd spent an hour fretting and pacing when they hadn't come home. She had fretted and paced plenty before when Michael had come home later than he'd predicted, but she had never fretted and paced about her folks.

The harsh knock on the door produced a uniformed state trooper who delivered the news like a telegram messenger during World War II. It took maybe thirty seconds for him to tell her that, in essence, her life was over.

"Unfortunately, two of them passed," he had said after describing the state of the "vehicle."

"Passed what?" she asked. He needed to be clearer.

"Your husband and your mother didn't make it."

"Are you saying they died?" she said. "You need to say it then."

She was mad. She was really upset.

The trooper, who was maybe twenty-five, asked if there was someone she could call, and did she want him to stay until they came? Yes, and no, she would rather wait alone, she said. It's not like she wanted to sit down and have tea and cookies with him. He hurried to the door. At least he hadn't sung the news: *Da-da da da da dah: Your husband and mom are dead.* She and Bobby had loved that joke when they were little.

And Philip years later.

The children were asleep upstairs. Mark, her obedient four-year-old, and Julie, her six-month-old baby. Julie had diarrhea and had been running a fever that evening and the pediatrician insisted they give her Pedialyte in addition to baby aspirin. That was why they were driving to the pharmacy in the storm. Her dad had offered to keep Michael company, and her mother went too.

The *what ifs* began. What if Jules hadn't been sick? What if they had waited to consult with the doctor? Or what if they had called the doctor earlier, so that conditions on the road had been better when the three set out on their trip? What if the doctor hadn't pushed the Pedialyte? What if her parents hadn't come up north for her surprise birthday party? Then only Michael would have driven to the pharmacy and not have been distracted by her mother's incessant blabbing.

Why had her mother joined them on that outing anyhow? This was something Caroline had always wanted to ask her because it seemed like overkill; no doubt Michael would have enjoyed a break from her parents to drive to CVS alone. Certainly, her dad's company would have been enough. Why had her mother gone too? And why had Michael taken the Parkway to the drugstore? It was a shortcut, but only saved a few minutes. Another thing. Why was her dad the only one wearing his seatbelt that slick, perilous night?

When she revisited that evening—over and over—she felt guilty that she hadn't called Bobby first, but when the officer asked if she had anyone to help out, it was Jean who came to mind. Jean was her best friend, and Jean was like an aunt to the kids.

"Drive incredibly slowly and carefully!" Caroline had shrieked over the phone to Jean after summoning her, and her friend was there in minutes. While waiting, Caroline had called her brother.

"There's been a terrible accident. Mom and Michael are dead. Dad's in critical condition," she said.

"Oh, my God. I'm on my way, Caroline. Are you okay? Stay there. I'm coming."

He lived in Philadelphia, two hours away.

"No, wait till morning. Please, Bobby. It's horrendous outside.

My girlfriend's coming. And promise me you'll drive slowly. It doesn't matter when you get here, just please be careful."

Or something like that she had said.

"I'll be careful," her brother said, his voice cracking.

◉ ◉ ◉

Bobby was an artist whose day job was as a printer. At his shop in Philly, he trained hard-to-hire young people. A few stayed to help him run his store, and he was successful at placing the others after they apprenticed with him, although he bemoaned how many print shops were closing in the city.

"People have stopped printing. They do everything on screens," he said.

Their mom had identified Bobby as an artist when he was seven and brought home a watercolor of a man with a spear. The tree in the foreground was intricately detailed while the warrior was more suggestive than representative, which Bernice deemed innovative for a child that age. She hung the painting in their front hall with other favorites, beautifully framed posters of Winslow Homer, Rembrandt, and Sargent.

Her brother had designed a noir cover for one of Caroline's novels, *Interior Demolition*. It depicted an empty road in the center of which sat an outsized typewriter with blood dripping down the side of its carriage. Her editor rejected it, saying, "It doesn't fit your story, at all. It's not like you've written a murder mystery."

"No, but I've written a book about a writer who wishes she could write a murder mystery—if she weren't such a scaredy-cat," Caroline replied. "Plus, I've put my lifeblood into this book."

She forced herself to accompany Bobby to identify the bodies, which thankfully turned out to be a formality less harrowing than the scenes depicted in homicide detective shows. They weren't brought inside a chilly morgue where someone pulled out a long drawer that contained their loved one with an identification tag hanging from an exposed big toe and a gauzy shroud over the rest of them, which would be rolled back to expose their scary, swollen face. Instead, they were ushered into a comfortable private room and shown photographs—one of Bernice's whole head, which was cut and bruised, but not grotesque, and one of the left side of Michael's face where he had a distinctive oval-shaped mole.

Even though she was not shown their most graphic injuries, Caroline's wavy hair went poker straight a few days after the accident. And stayed that way for months.

◉ ◉ ◉

Caroline had always run scared. Even before the very worst happened, she had worried about losing people prematurely. *Please God, bless everyone I love, and they love, and don't let anything happen to them,* had been her nightly prayer until her worst fears came true. Afterwards, *Drive slowly. Be safe. Don't rush* became her mantra. But though she felt she would jinx people's travels if she didn't caution them, she also worried she would jinx them if she did. So, she settled on *Have a good trip.*

After the accident, she developed more *checking behaviors,* as her therapist labeled them: Were all the lights off, doors closed and locked, gas off, heat down, faucets tightened? And she was on prevent mode. She kept a copy of all her credit cards in a filing cabinet at home, and brought her keys and wallet when she went out with Philip in case he lost his.

Philip waited years for her to ease up. He planned trips, most with the kids, occasionally for the two of them. She tried to enjoy them, but she spent a lot of the time counting the hours until they would go home, longing to return to what? Had she felt she could keep everyone safer at home? That the longer they stayed away, the more likely the shoe would drop?

In her grief-counseling group, which that young trooper had left her a pamphlet about, she met Lisa. She too had been through the mill, arguably worse than Caroline, if comparing one's tragedies wasn't also apples versus oranges. Lisa's brother had died in Vietnam when she was in college. Later, she had worked as a travel agent and booked a flight to California for her father and her aunt after their brother, Lisa's uncle, died of a mysterious virus there. Their plane went down over Shanksville, Pennsylvania on 9/11. Her dad and aunt had died while flying to a funeral! A few years later, Lisa's mother committed suicide.

"You don't get over any of it, ever," Lisa had counseled Caroline, although she was there to be counseled too.

"But how are you not cowering in a corner somewhere, completely devastated and afraid?" Caroline asked, her face covered in tears.

"I refuse to live in fear," Lisa said. "I keep busy, that's how you deal." Lisa had become a tax accountant, which kept her hectic between January and mid-April, and busy otherwise. "I don't leave time to dwell on what I've lost," she had said.

"Do you still fly?" Caroline asked.

"I don't see flying as risky. In a way, I'm more sanguine about everything, I guess because I believe I've already seen the worst. I feel less vulnerable, more willing to take risks. I don't sweat anything anymore. Big deal if something goes wrong. Last year, I planned my daughter's wedding with zero stress. Whatever happens, happens."

Oh, give me a break, Caroline had thought. For one thing, she would grieve longer for her losses. For another, Caroline had never wanted to be so busy that she couldn't think or feel. In fact, her predilection was to slow things down. Philip called her a world-class putterer, but world-class ponderer was more apropos. That was when she got her best ideas.

Still, during this time she couldn't write. The grief counselors advocated journaling, and for those who didn't routinely pick up a pen, it seemed to help. Before, Caroline had never stopped writing; even when away from her desk, she was constantly jotting down descriptions, conversation snippets, and plot twists. After the accident, some suggested she had more to write about than ever, which seemed callous.

She thought about dying every day of her life.

Her young kids had saved her. She had to smile for them, even if she was faking it, or they would never learn to smile. She had to play with them, read to them, and tell them upbeat stories because she wanted them to have happy stories of their own. She was somewhat better when they were around.

But she couldn't bring herself to shop or eat out, two activities that had previously given her great pleasure. When she did get in the car, she drove slowly, hoping lights would turn red before she reached them. She had observed others driving like this in the past. Now she knew why. Time crawled. And she couldn't write. If she found out she was terminal, it would almost be a relief, she had thought more than—

"Oh, give us a break. Can we get back to the present? Earth to Caroline."

◉ ◉ ◉

That was one of Philip's expressions, but it is Michael ghost talking, or rather Michael ghost's voice, from up above, near the kitchen chandelier. While she has always thought they were diametrically different, her two husbands share a corny sense of humor and some pet phrases. *We know what we like,* Caroline

muses, just as she has purchased variations of the same shirt and sweater for years.

"That's some maudlin stuff, Caroline," the cloud says. It is still Michael, but he is now in the shape of a bright white, bulbous cloud, unfettered to his in-laws—her parents—for once. Hallelujah that!

"You don't want to know," she says to the cloud. "I was a wreck at first—no pun intended. But I got better over time. Raising kids can be very distracting, all-consuming really. And Philip has been so wonderful. Perhaps Philip most of—"

"I guess you can't sleep," Michael says with a peevish tone.

"Duh," she says. "This is a lot to take in." Caroline looks up at the wall clock; a few more hours till sunrise. She sips her ginger tea, but it has gotten cold. "Why is it you're chained to my parents anyhow, and not *your* mother and maybe her sister— you know, your crazy Aunt Doris?"

The cloud shape turns gray. "As I've said, repeatedly, sweetie, we don't get many explanations where we come from."

"I was thinking it's because you were all observant Jews. Oh my God—um, goodness—you don't know this, sweetie, but your mother ended up converting at the end. She became Episcopalian, like your dad."

The cloud gets grayer. "I did hear something about that. But it was only because she was dying, right? I'm sure she thought that's what my dad wanted, and maybe she thought it would help them be together in the hereafter. I'm not certain it will though. The rules are very fuzzy." He sighs. "I've always assumed I'm with your folks because I was the one behind the wheel that night. I'm responsible for their lives—or rather deaths—along with my own."

"So, it's your fate to care for them for eternity? That's ridiculous. And speaking of rules, didn't you say you weren't allowed downstairs?"

"Well, it seems I'm able to be a cloud in your kitchen—but only when you're here alone."

"The accident wasn't deemed your fault, Michael. You need to know that at least. The roads were treacherous that night, really icy and slippery. Remember?" She sips the cold tea. "What did happen anyway?"

"I lost control of the vehicle, Caroline."

"Could you have fallen asleep?"

"You mean during one of your mom's soliloquies?"

Caroline laughs. "That was one of my theories too. But maybe you just got distracted. You could get pretty spacey when you drove."

"Look who's talking," Michael says.

"Speaking of Mom, it's weird. She's almost taciturn now in comparison."

"Give it a bit. She's winding up. She'll get there." The cloud swirls. "I'd had a beer that night, you know."

"You did? I wasn't sure. Still, one beer never knocked you out. Listen, I don't believe it was your fault. No one's ever said that."

"To your face."

"No." She reaches up to touch the airy cloud on the ceiling and it flattens out. She sighs. "Hey, by the way, how do you know the expression 'Earth to Caroline'? I'm pretty sure that came into parlance after your demise."

The cloud inflates and shakes vigorously, like it's being tickled. "Oh, you mean, not from way back when we used words like *parlance* and *demise*? But I think you're wrong. 'Earth to whomever' is an oldie, but goody. We absolutely used it way back when. Anyway, regardless, I've come to fetch you. Would you please get out of your own sorry way and join the party in the attic? We have *a lot* of catching up to do and your folks await."

CHAPTER FIVE

You may attend a party where strange customs prevail.
—fortune cookie

The attic is ablaze! Michael has plugged in all the spare lights stored up there: desk lamps, nightstand lamps, swing-arm lamps, torchieres. Caroline has a thing about just the right lighting.

"At last!" Bernice says, turning away from a full-length, dust-covered mirror before which she's been primping. "Where ya been? We don't have a lifetime here, you know. Haha. That's a good one."

Now this sounds more like good ole mom. "You're back," Caroline says.

"We've been waiting and waiting. It's you who are back. We've been here," Bernice says.

"Whose back?" Norman says.

Caroline stares at her parents. "I'm sorry, but I have to spend time downstairs too. I've got a husband, and guests arriving in a few hours."

"A new husband, tsk, tsk," Bernice says.

Norman motions for Caroline to lean toward him and whispers, "Mom's out shopping. She'll be home by suppertime."

"I'm right here, Norm."

Her father smiles at Caroline. "I just got back from Chicago, big trip, went very well. I think she's planning a welcome home dinner. That'll be interesting. She doesn't cook as much as she used to, the old gal."

"I'll bet," Caroline says. She turns to Michael, "Is this because of his head injury, because of the crash?"

Michael nods. "And it's a shame because, where we come from, we're told that, all things being equal, our brains will stop aging at eighty, meaning they won't deteriorate further after that. So that's one good thing about dying on the younger side." He lowers his voice to a whisper, "In your dad's case, he's in and out," then louder, "but for most people, once you die, brain decay stops when you reach eighty whereas, if you don't die until you're over eighty, you're stuck with whatever brain capacity you have when you die. So, it's a tradeoff, but still better to live past eighty, in my opinion."

Caroline's fifty-nine-year-old brain can barely digest this. *Why is Michael the only one in color?* she wonders. He has assumed his normal shape again and is back to sitting smushed between her old-but-don't-look-so-old, black-and-white folks.

"That's bizarre," Caroline mumbles. "Hey, I need to ask you something, sweetie. How long have you been able to read my thoughts? And please don't tell me since the accident."

"No, no. If that were true, I'd know a hell of a lot more, right? Only since we arrived here. And only when we're in the same room."

"Thank God."

"Why?" he asks. "Are we keeping secrets?"

"You look nice, Caroline," Bernice says.

"Thanks. Really? My hair's receding."

"But you still have those great waves. You really can't tell."

"That's nice of you to say."

"Well, it's true. I think you've aged well, very well."

"I have to tell you, you're blowing my mind, Mom, with all these compliments. What happened to your ultra-critical self up there?"

"I was hardly ultra-critical, Caroline. That's cruel."

"It's true!"

"Girls," Norman says softly.

"Ladies!" Michael corrects him. "Enough."

"You're giving me a pain in my knickers, Bernice," Norman says.

He has always taken Caroline's side, so she appeals to him now. "It's not really fair, the way mom's acting now . . . out of the wild-blue yonder. For years I've fantasized that, if I ever saw her again, which I'd always imagined would be at some lovely bar in heaven with her favorite Cole Porter tune playing, and Cosmos flowing freely—although that's not the picture you guys are painting of heaven so far. In fact, I'm not getting much of a picture at all."

"Well, it sure ain't like that, what you were thinking, I'm tellin' ya." Bernice sings:

The things that you're liable

To read in the Bible

It ain't—

"Mom!" Caroline faces her mother. "I've dreamed of the chance to see you again so we could talk . . . not sing. Because, when you died, things weren't so good between us. Remember?"

Bernice looks surprised.

"Come on! We were fighting the night you died, and I for one have regretted that we didn't have a chance to make up, even though I'm no longer positive what the fight was about."

"We weren't fighting, dear."

"We absolutely were. I remember you screaming at me."

"I'm not a screamer, Caroline."

"Mom."

"We were there for your birthday. What reason would we have to fight?"

"If I had to guess, you were going on about my mothering. You thought I was too attentive to the kids, too responsive to their needs. Too indulgent, you used to say, or something like that. You were super judgmental. But maybe it wasn't as big a fight as I thought if neither of us remembers the specifics."

"I don't remember us fighting," Bernice says. "But if I had to guess, you were making us feel guilty about moving to Asheville."

"I really don't think so."

"Why not?" Bernice asks.

"Because I was way past that by then."

And this is why she doesn't like to revisit things with her mother, who always has an alternate reality in which she, Bernice, is the victim.

"Anyway, it doesn't matter. What I've wanted to tell you for so long, Mom, is that I've had a sea change."

"About what?"

"Everything! I mean, I struggled with your constant criticism and felt a lot of it was unfair. But after all this time, I try to appreciate your good qualities. I'm old enough to realize we do the best we can, even if we fall short. And now you've returned as a saint, or angel, or whatever, I guess to cement a better reputation for posterity. Is that it? You're trying to reshape your legacy by being so agreeable?" Caroline bites her lips. Her intention is to reconcile.

The ghosts sit transfixed, and Michael has lost most of the color he'd gained, although Bernice turns the color of fire. "You could always dole it out, Caroline," she says.

"What? I'm trying to say something nice here. I'm trying to tell you that—"

Bernice sings:

Sue me, sue me

Blah, blah, blah-blah me

"Mom! I'm trying to tell you I've made peace with it all because I realize you learned at Grandma's knees. She was hard on you, and you were hard on me. I wish I had defended myself more, but you've provided a useful negative role model for raising my own kids. I try to do the opposite, especially with Julie—not be so quick to criticize and judge."

A black puff of smoke emerges from the top of Bernice's head. "I'm sure you've been perfect," she says.

"I'm not saying that, and we've had plenty of friction, but I'm not always coming down on her. Anyway, now that I'm getting the chance I never thought I'd have, what I'm trying to say is that, while I remember your critical ways, I try to appreciate the good things you did for me instead, like giving me a love of literature, and music, all kinds of music. And art and—"

"Say, that's pretty good."

"You're right. It is." And to be fair, there was something else. Her mother had boosted her confidence in her appearance, had been very sweet that way. She recalled a time when they were getting ready to attend her grandparents' fiftieth anniversary party and Caroline discovered at the eleventh hour that she had outgrown the outfit she'd planned to wear. Bernice had loaned Caroline the dress she had bought for herself for the occasion.

Caroline smiles at her mother. "I do think I inherited your hypochondria, though."

"You're a hypochondriac?"

"What about the terrible pain in my right side?"
Caroline had asked her gastroenterologist recently.

"It gets less concerning with every passing year," he
had replied. "You might want to cut down on wine, and
coffee."

Not what she wanted to hear.

"Still go out for coffee every morning?" Michael asks, in her
head again.

They had met in a strip-mall parking lot one beautiful May
morning when she'd walked smack into the rear of his car
because she was running late for work. She was home from
graduate school for the summer, working as a temp, and she
was so intent on reaching the Dunkin' Donuts and getting her
coffee that she hadn't noticed the car she was walking behind
had come to a stop. A handsome guy jumped out when he felt
the thump.

"You need to look where you're going!" His pick-up line.

"How come I don't get to read *your* mind?" Caroline asks
Michael-the-ghost now.

"There are things we need to tell you too, dear," Bernice
says, employing a sweet tone again. "But if you really want to
hear about heaven, I'll tell you about that first. Actually, we're
not convinced we are in heaven, are we guys? It's more like
purgatory, bordering on hell."

"It's like a giant shopping mall," Norman says, "that you're
in forever. You know how they disguise the exits?"

"It's certainly not what it's made out to be," Bernice
continues. "We get mostly junk food to eat, but I've heard in
the real heaven, they eat very sensibly, just a few sweets in
moderation, and they feel better, think more clearly." Bernice
looks at Norman. "And last longer."

"Takes one to know one," Norman says.

"They also get more travel privileges," Michael says. "But we're not in purgatory, let alone hell, Bernice. We're in heaven, just kind of on a lower deck, but on the waitlist to move up. It all depends on how we collectively comport ourselves." He notices Norman has nodded off again.

"We're making the best of it," Bernice says. "You should be proud of us. You said yourself that I've kept my girlish figure. And we get a lot of rest, and not much stress." She leans forward. "Speaking of stress, I need to tell you something, dear. But first you must sit. Pull up a chair. It's about your father, and we think it's urgent you know."

Caroline unfolds a bridge chair and sits facing her three ghosts. "What about him?"

"Well, to cut to the chase, he's not really your father." She nudges Norman, but he doesn't stir.

"Haha," Caroline says, but something about her mother's expression makes her add, "What are you talking about? What do you mean?"

"It's a shocker, I know, but hear me out. I'm talking biologically only. In every other way of course he's been your father, full-heartedly, no holds barred. It's just that he, Norman, was bitten in the crotch by a ferocious dog when he was a teenager, and his testicles were badly damaged. He could still perform, you know, but had no real sperm to speak of, no good swimmers and—"

"Stop it Mom!"

"I'm sorry. We never felt a need to tell you because, for all intents and purposes, he is your real father." Bernice squeezes Norman's hand and for the first time his skin turns pink.

Caroline stands and kisses her father's translucent forehead. Cold and slimy. "He's been the best, an awesome father," she says.

"Yeah, yeah, that's why we never wanted to tell you the backstory 'cause for all intents and—"

"So, why are you telling me now?"

"He never wanted you to know, but it's just, we've heard about all the DNA tests people are doing these days—23 and you, Me, and Him, or whatever they're called—and we thought we better let you know before you decide to do one."

"Wait—you're serious? I don't believe this! And how about Bobby? Do we have the same father at least? Say yes."

Bernice beams. "Yup, you do. Your Uncle Bruce was the donor, both times. That's why you're such a close match to Norman—you're almost his child genetically, almost the same exact."

"Not really," Caroline says. "Uncle Bruce was chronically depressed, wasn't he? That's pretty different. Didn't Uncle Bruce kill himself? *He* was our father? I have to say I'm having a super hard time believing this. I think you're just saying it because I came down hard on you before. We've always had more bones to pick than I had with Dad. I know you begrudged our relationship."

"I might have been a little jealous at times, but I'm not making this up, Caroline. You said you wanted to know everything."

Caroline is silent.

"Uncle Bruce was a member of Menses, for Pete's sake!" Bernice says.

"*Mensa*, you mean," Caroline says.

"I said that."

"No—"

"Ahem," Michael says, placing his index finger to his lips, telling her to stop.

Whatever. Caroline ponders. Memory is a crazy thing, how you kind of know something on some level, but not fully, how you might question something, but not truly grasp its significance until you learn something else, perhaps, as in this instance, much later. Growing up, she had often wondered how it was that she and Bobby had light eyes when both of their parents—or both people they thought were their parents—had brown? She isn't sure she remembers her tenth (or eleventh) grade biology lessons correctly, but didn't you need one parent with non-brown eyes to pass on non-brown eyes to your children? Or, at the least, even if both brown-eyed parents had the recessive eye-color gene, wouldn't it be rare, statistically speaking, for both children to come out with non-brown eyes? Unlike Norman, Uncle Bruce of Mensa had green eyes!

She turns to Michael for support and now sees black puffs coming out of the top of his head. "Your Uncle Bruce killed himself? How is it you never told me that, sweetie?"

"I'm sure I told you. You definitely knew," Caroline says, but he is angry.

"Okay, Michael, your turn," Bernice says. "Isn't there something you want to tell Caro—"

"Your Uncle Bruce killed himself?" an intruder asked.

⊙ ⊙ ⊙

"Whoa. You scared me!" Caroline is startled to see Philip at the top of the attic steps, frowning. He is a stealth operative, and he looks pissed.

"I never knew that's how he died. That's terrible. And you're still wrangling with your mom? Let it go already. You have to let it all go, Caroline."

"Nice pjs," Michael ghost says.

"Who is he?" Norman asks.

"How long have you been standing there?" Caroline asks. Philip is wearing light blue pajamas with white piping. She had bought them for him.

"Long enough to be worried," Philip said.

"No, really."

"I came in on, 'Didn't Uncle Bruce kill himself?' Really, Caroline, what's going on? Who are you talking to? What exactly are you doing?"

She's dumbfounded. The ghosts remain in their chairs before her, but Philip can neither see nor hear them: her former husband, her mom, and the man she's always called Dad. She is shaking. *Must regroup.*

"I'm not talking to anyone, obviously. I'm rehearsing a play I've written. I'm using real names for now, but it's fiction, or at least my special brand. I really didn't hear you come up."

"Why do you keep sneaking up here?" Philip said.

"You already asked me that."

"Why aren't you sleeping? Why are you always out of breath? And—" He handed her the blue note he had found on her night table. "Where is this from? Who wrote it?"

One banana. Two banana. Three banana. Presto!

Philip saw the lightbulb go off in her head.

"This? Oh, that's ancient history," she says. "I mean, you can see that's one old piece of paper." She tries to formulate a story. "I found it up here. It's, you know, from before."

"It doesn't look that old," Philip said.

She looks into his eyes. "Well, it is. You have to take my word. It's just been pickled in the attic." Deep breaths. "It's from the night of the accident, Philip." Yes, this might work, and she comforts herself because the paper itself *is* very old. Has to be. Michael is long dead, and this is one of his light blue sheets, and he certainly isn't reordering stationery in heaven. So, this part is true. Also, she found the note in the attic where Michael ghost had left it for her, so that is true too.

But it isn't from before—he just wrote it—and it was careless of her to leave it on her night table. She hates lying to Philip.

She lies or exaggerates a lot to get out of things or make stories better, an occupational hazard. But she has never lied to Philip—until now. *Michael is making me do it!* "He must have written it before he got into the car that night, before they went off on that fateful joy ride."

"*'Take care of your dishes?'* That's what preoccupied him, your doing the dishes? And why are they your dishes anyhow? Didn't he help out?"

The note refers to her present Thanksgiving meal preparations, of course, not her job to clean the dishes, but she has no choice but to continue with her fabrication. "I think we had more traditional roles than you and I. Michael didn't do many dishes, I can tell you that. He wasn't helpful, like you."

"*Hey! Yes I was!*" *says a voice only she can hear.* "*That's not fair.*"

Caroline maintains her focus. "I was upstairs with the baby—with Julie—when they left for the store that night and he left this note. She was very sick, you know the story. I didn't even realize they'd gone at first, or that my mother had gone with them." She looks at the note again and can't resist a further embellishment. "It's ironic that he said, 'We'll be back,' don't you think?" She starts to cry.

Philip hugged her for a long moment. "What's with the chairs? Having a party?"

She smiles. "More like a meeting. I hope you'll be able to attend sometime. Let me just say goodbye to my guests." Caroline turns back to the three. "Sorry, guys, it's only fair I spend some time downstairs with my great husband, whom I hope you'll get to meet soon."

As she talks, the ghosts fade away.

"*We'll be back in the morning,*" she hears Michael say, though her three visitors are once again gone.

Philip, who had been rolling his eyes during his wife's

theatrical goodbye to the three empty chairs, now gave her a big smile. "Very funny."

She took his hand. This time, she pulled him over to the steps.

He pointed to the skylight. "Look at that moon. It's so full, so orange."

The attic has many moods, Philip thought. Through the skylight, they might see clouds that looked like dense, creamy mountains or fast-moving, scattered clouds high up in the heavens. And the light changed with the seasons, running a gamut of colors: crème, quinoa, and take-five blue, to channel the stack of paint-sample cards he had on his desk.

"How late is it?" Caroline asked.

"Plenty late. Almost dawn."

⦿ ⦿ ⦿

Whenever Caroline was worried or concerned, her counting mind appeared. *1, 2, 3,* counting steps; *1 to 5,* counting flights of stairs. Her counting mind was triggered when she couldn't sleep, reviewing the multiplication tables for 8's and 9's, or ticking off a sequence as she laid on her left side and moved her right foot in a large circle against the crisp sheets: *1, 2, 3, 1; 1, 2, 3, 2; 1, 2, 3, 3* . . . Or starting at 200 and counting backwards by 7's. This exercise invariably lulled her to sleep—crowding out other thoughts, creative, anxious, or otherwise. Only backwards by 7's worked because other numbers had simple patterns, like *191, 182, 173* for 9's. So, she did 7's, and although she just about knew them backwards by heart now, she didn't quite, so the exercise still soothed and relaxed her: *193, 186, 179, 172.* At *151,* she might check her accuracy: *200-151 = 49* and *49 = 7x7. Good!* It got more challenging as she progressed: *81 + 119 = 200,* and *119* is *17 x 7.* Right! She could still divide like that in her head, and she could put people to sleep just describing these methods.

"You like numbers," Philip had observed, and, for a right brain thinker, it was odd, but true, that she was fascinated by them. To Caroline, numbers were magical.

She stopped counting. Hmm. If they learned so little where they came from, how did her parents know about DNA tests? And how did Michael *hear* his mom had converted to Christianity as she lay dying when that had taken place eight years after he was killed in a car crash?

CHAPTER SIX

You will be sought out for your diplomatic skills.
—fortune cookie

Thanksgiving Day, the third major Jewish holiday, as Mark proclaimed it, and unequivocally his favorite. "Let the heavens rumble and the mountains roar," he called out as he crossed the threshold of the front door. "Holy Hosanna, your prodigal son is here at last." The house was super quiet.

"Guys? Hello?" Mark peered into the kitchen. "Yoo-hoo. Where are you?" Smells overwhelmed him: sweet potatoes with ginger, smoked turkey, corn casserole, wild mushroom soup with sherry. Lots and lots of dishes, and most of them somewhat sweet. It was like *Fantasia!*

It wasn't even noon, but everything was ready. Of course. His mother was an early bird, a planner, and unfalteringly prompt as well—except maybe this morning. "Hel-lo? Anyone?"

Some welcome. He checked the living room, kitchen, and den, then hoisted his weekend bag over his shoulder and headed upstairs to his old room, taking a detour to use the bathroom. After that, he shut the hatch to the attic, surprised to see it ajar. His dad had said she'd been subsumed by the attic again, cleaning and sorting, he guessed. Although his mom often lamented that it was hard to confront the past, she sure loved to rearrange it. He pulled the stairs halfway down in case she was up there, and yelled, "Your majesty? Anyone here?" Silence.

A whiff of cold air passed over him as he stood in the upstairs hall, so he checked the bathroom window and the ones in his bedroom. All shut tight. Weird. His room seemed so tidy in contrast to his apartment. And all his stuff was gone. She had told him she was on a tear. An armada of Lego pirate ships stood alone on the bookshelves. He examined the little pirates on their decks, remembering how Julie had tormented him by removing their tiny hands and hooks.

Another cool breeze, coming from where? Then he heard his mom's voice and moved just outside his parents' bedroom door.

"Oh, that's just peachy. And I must say I've never been called babe by a blob before, or blotch, or splotch, or whatever you're supposed to be. Haha yourself. But I do still love that giggle of yours, sweetie. I've missed it. And, no matter what you say, you just don't seem like you're in your early sixties now, physically or mentally. I don't believe you've been aging all this time."

His mother's tone was unfamiliar, flirtatious, never mind that she was standing in her closet, talking to the ceiling. It was not unusual for her to talk to herself, but this seemed different. He squeezed into the closet behind her, gripped her shoulders. "Mama-la, hi. I'm afraid to ask, but who are you talking to?"

Caroline jumped before turning toward him, her face flushed as she hugged him hard. "Mark, you're here. I'm so glad." She released him and trained her eyes upward again. "This is Mark," she informed the ceiling.

"Very funny. Uh, everything all right?" he asked. "You look strange, and you're so winded."

She stared at him. "Why does everyone keep saying that? I'm just trying to figure out what to wear."

"You were talking to the ceiling!"

"You've grown a beard. I like it. It has some red in it, and it's fuller than last time." She reached out to touch his beard, but he moved her hand away.

"Mom?"

"I'm fine, no stranger than usual. Well, I've got this ghost thing going on."

"What?"

She laughed. "I'm going after this ghostly, ghastly, look."

"You look fine. But were you talking to the old dad just now?"

She tensed. "The old dad? Why would you say that?"

A draft of cold air passed over Mark again and he hugged his arms to his chest. "I don't know. You sounded different. It's freezing in here, by the way."

Following his mom's gaze upward, he noticed how messed up the ceiling was, as if a major amount of water had leaked from the attic, leaving a bulbous splotch that seemed organic in some indescribable way. It twitched or pulsated for a second and then flattened out.

"Yuck. What happened in here?" Mark pointed to the splotch.

"We'll get it fixed. Never you mind."

"Never you mind?" He kept his eyes on the splotch. "Where could the water be coming from? Isn't the attic above this? No water up there last time I looked."

His mother took his hand and pulled him into the bedroom. "Where's Dad?" she asked.

"I have no idea. I couldn't find him. Mom, what happened to your closet?"

"He must be downstairs. I left him watching a game. Nice haircut, by the way." He had her waves whereas Julie's hair was straight.

"Thanks, appreciate it, but—"

She took his hand again. "Let's go down."

"You're not going to explain?"

"I can't."

"Why not? Please?"

"Okay, you know I like to pretend. I'm trying my hand at a play and that bizarre splotch gives me all sorts of ideas. You caught me working out a scene."

"Seriously? Well, I hope we don't have a flood. It's nasty looking. You have to get it fixed." His dad used to be all over home repairs, but apparently not anymore. Mark had tripped over a dislodged paver on the front walk and several tiles in the hall bathroom were cracked.

"Is Julie coming?" his mom asked.

"How should I know?"

"We don't know either. She didn't RSVP. She's being very secretive."

"That was part of her request, right? Although I think it's ridiculous that you're funding her through this. She needs to grow up already. You need to take a firmer stand."

"Like tough love? Are you going into family therapy?"

"That's the thing. I'm a kid and it's obvious to me this isn't being handled well."

"Philip?" his mom called out. "Honey, where are you? Mark's here."

The back door slammed. "Honey?" Philip shouted.

Jupiter barked.

"Mark's here!"

"Mark who?"

Mark and Caroline laughed.

"Ugh, the thing is, I find myself making the same corny jokes," he said.

⊙ ⊙ ⊙

In the redolent kitchen, Mark sat at the counter with his father while his mom served him hot chocolate with pastel-colored baby marshmallows, like he was a little kid again, not that he was complaining. Jupiter had managed to squeeze into the space by their legs and was sleeping with her head on Mark's shoe. Tufts of black and white fur clung to Mark's black pants.

"I'm thinking of giving notice at the end of the year," he said.

"Why would you do that?" Caroline asked.

"I'm tired of this job. It's drudge work, mind-numbing, and it's clearly not—"

"Getting you anywhere?"

He shook his head. "I feel like I'm already stuck, and I just started. It's super bureaucratic, and my boss is an asshole. And I just don't like PR. I have some money saved. I want to go to South America, travel for a while, and find—"

"Yourself?" Caroline asked.

"Mom, stop interrupting!"

"I'm sorry. You know I love to finish sentences."

"I was going to say, I want to figure out other things I'm suited for."

"Like David Copperfield. But in South America."

"I just need—"

"A time-out?"

"Mom!"

"I'm sorry, I'm sorry. Occupational hazard." One of many. "Julie calls her current experiment a time-out."

"I have the money," Mark said.

His mother whacked a metal spoon on the counter. "I think it's a terrible idea. It's hard to be entry level, I get that, but you're only twenty-three, for God's sake, and this job could be a great stepping stone. You can't just go wandering."

"I can, Mom. I can use some of the money Grandpa Spencer put aside for me. I haven't touched it."

"But you'll need it later!"

Philip's cell phone rang and he excused himself.

◉ ◉ ◉

"Listen to me, Philip," Ted said. "Just hear me out."

It was hard to hear at all. It sounded like Ted was calling from a war zone.

"I need the money more than you, and it's not fair that you've been making me continue to pay the firm's carrying costs."

"*Your* share of the firm's costs. And by the way, we're partners, Ted. We have a contract!"

Ted hung up.

◉ ◉ ◉

"Who was that?" Caroline asked as Philip reentered the kitchen.

"Ted."

"Ted Eskin?"

"The very same. He's in trouble."

Caroline rolled her eyes. "He *is* trouble," she said. The last time they spent an evening with Ted and his wife, he had greeted Caroline at the door with a kiss on the lips and tried to thrust his tongue down her throat. "What kind of trouble?" she asked, but Philip just shook his head and his eyes signaled, *We'll talk later*.

"Dad—I was telling Mom, I won't need a lot of money," Mark continued. "South America's cheap. That's part of the point. It's really cheap, I've heard."

"You'd go by yourself? I'm not crazy about that either," Caroline said.

"I'm twenty-three, and I traveled by myself a lot in Australia. I know what I'm doing."

His mother set the spoon down. Brisket sauce dripped down

her white blouse. "I just don't see why you have to do it now," she said. "This isn't a good time."

"If not now, when, as they say?" Mark said.

"Why aren't you saying anything, Philip?"

Philip looked up from his reverie. He had been fighting back tears, so unlike him. Were it not for Ted, they would have managed financially, he was thinking. Things would have been okay. "Let the record show I've been listening," he said, straightening in his chair. "It's true what he says, honey. It will get harder and harder to take a decent amount of time off when he's older." Compartmentalizing!

"Exactly," Mark said, smiling at his dad as his mom whacked the spoon again. "And you know what, Mom? If you're going to overreact every time I tell you something, I'm not going to discuss my plans with you. But I don't think you'd like that either, right?"

"Right," Caroline said with a sheepish smile.

"Aw, c'mon. Don't look so sad. I'm not talking about forever. I'm just out of school. I can afford a little detour."

"So, what do you envision? How much time?" Philip asked.

"I don't know. Five months? Consider it another experiment. You went along with Julie's."

Now Philip frowned. "I'm sorry to have to tell you this, but there's not a hell of a lot in that account because we needed it for your tuition at the end, when you took the extra semester. We told you at the time. Your grandfather intended it to help fund college, but we were able to cover all your other semesters ourselves."

"But there's some left, right, Dad? I don't need much. I've saved a little on my own. I really want to do this."

"There isn't much, and it might be good to keep that as a cushion," Philip said. "It's nice to have a cushion."

Caroline placed her palms on Mark's shoulders and smiled. "Okay, listen. I'm speaking calmly now, but you know what? This isn't a great time for this discussion."

"Why not? I'm here. I'm home."

"Because a lot's going on. And we have to get ready."

Something banged overhead.

"What's that?" Philip and Mark asked together.

"Boxes? Toppling boxes? It doesn't matter. I'll deal with them later," Caroline said. "We have to get ready."

"You're ready!" Mark said.

She pointed to her stained blouse.

"Your mom's exhausted," Philip said. "She hasn't been sleeping. We'll talk about it tomorrow."

"Fine," Mark said, stomping out of the room. "I'm not going to grabble."

"*Grovel*," Caroline corrected.

He shot her a look. "I'm taking a shower."

Once Mark reached the second floor, Philip confronted her. "I'll ask you again, Caroline. What's going on? It's obvious you're hiding something. You're acting strange. Mark feels it too."

"It's so bizarre. I'm having all these feelings, maybe it's the holidays? I don't know. I want to tell you more about it, I really do, but I can't just now. I'm not allowed."

"Not allowed? What does that mean? Why not?"

"Trust me, this is one of those times when you need to let it go. You know how we start to argue sometimes, and you say, 'Let it go. This one's not worth litigating,' so we drop it and that works out better? It's the same with this."

"Not really, because I say that about petty arguments. This seems bigger, stranger."

"You have to trust me—that I'm too tired and something prevents me from talking, sweetie. I mean honey."

Philip smiled. "I like when you call me sweetie."

"Sweetie's the guy in her play," Mark yelled from the upstairs hall.

The blob in her closet snickers.

Caroline kissed Philip. "Doesn't he get tired of being right all the time?"

CHAPTER SEVEN

Your ear for music is becoming more finely tuned.
—fortune cookie

She was taking a chance by running up to the attic one more time. It was getting late and time was running out—but time was of the essence, as they say. When not at her writing, her mind indulged in clichés. Their guests would arrive shortly, but Mark and Philip were ensconced in the den watching the Jets-Patriots game. They loved to root against the Patriots for some reason that never made sense to Caroline since Philip grew up near Boston. Whatever, they were content, and she was temporarily relieved of scrutiny. She needed to tell her ghostly cadre that she would be unavailable until late tonight and beg them to stick around. If they were compelled to go back, to wherever they went, they had to promise to return.

As she ascends the attic steps, Michael stares down at her. He is in technicolor and detached from her parents, momentarily free, like her, of the ties that bind. He's sniffling. When she reaches him, he yanks her over to the farthest corner of the huge attic space. In the early afternoon light, particles of dust dance before her eyes. Michael gestures to two bridge chairs he has set up and says, "Sit." His red, swollen eyes reveal he's been sobbing.

"Oh my God, Michael. What's wrong?" She's forgotten how emotional he can be, so different than Philip that way.

He wipes his eyes. "You've got your boating outfit on this evening," he says. "Where you going?"

"Off into the sunset." She has replaced her stained blouse with a jaunty blue and white striped cotton shirt. "You never liked stripes," she says.

Michael sighs. "Mark's so big! I mean, he's a grown man already. I don't know why I didn't realize it, but I've missed everything, Caroline. Don't get me wrong, he looks terrific, and it's all miraculous, but it's also devastating to tangibly see what I've lost out on while waiting for permission to visit. I've missed their whole lives!"

And then the wait.

Not long, I grant, but all my life.

"Richard Hugo?" Michael asks. His voice is loud. *Like Mark's,* she thinks.

"Galway Kinnell. I'm pretty sure."

He shrugs and hands her a baby journal, Mark's, which they had taken turns writing in throughout their son's first year. The outside is pink and blue to hedge all bets, with an inscription on the inside cover: "I can't wait to help you spoil little you-know-who to death." A gift from Bobby, who had put this journal together at his shop with his own sketches of baby animals at the top of each section and thin-ruled lines, the way Caroline liked them.

Michael guides her to a chair. "Listen to this," he whispers, taking the journal back from her and searching for a certain page. Her eyes dart to the far end of the long room, where she confirms that Mama and Papa Ghost remain precisely the way she left them hours before, slumped in their chairs against the wall.

"They can't be this tired! It's crazy, Michael. Listen to how loud she's snoring," Caroline says.

"They're old, Caroline, and not accustomed to travel. Listen to this."

Daddy and Mommy can't get over how wonderful you are. We strolled you to nearby Anderson Park today. Several neighbors came to peek at you, and Rich across the street said, "What a great-looking kid." Everyone admires your size. You are long and filled out and can hold your head better than most newborns. Your first outing was on a lovely, sunny Saturday. The leaves have turned.

You were dressed in a cotton gown with colorful rocking horses on it and white knee socks, which made you look like Mercury Martin, a famous soccer player who always wore his sweat socks really high.

"You wrote that," she says. "I remember those socks and you telling me about Mercury Martin. In some ways, it doesn't seem that long ago."

"I have to spend time with him, Caroline. They must let me." He sniffles.

She wipes her eyes and sniffles too. "You are such a mush. I loved that about you."

"I don't know my son at all," he says. "Did he become a genius? Remember when he took that stacking toy apart with those rubber rings, and sorted them into piles by color? Four different colors and he did it perfectly. He was like, what, ten months old? We were in awe."

She has forgotten about that, too. "Remember how sweet he was, Michael, how good? My friends still say he was the cutest little kid ever. He picked up on adult cues so fast, and he was so polite."

"Yeah, yeah," Michael says. "We already reminisced about that. I want to hear the rest of his story."

So, she tells him.

"I guess we asked a lot of him because he was so easy, and he was our first. We were always on him about everything, held him to such high standards. I realized this more as Julie got older. We were too demanding of Mark, too exacting, while with Julie we really had to pick our battles. Not that Philip and I weren't strict with her too. I think you would have approved our level of discipline.

"But, you know, even though he was so great with adults, he was reticent with kids. Which was okay in elementary school—he had a few friends and got straight A's. In retrospect, I feel bad because maybe I didn't praise him enough for his grades because Julie struggled so much in school from the get-go, and I didn't want her to feel bad. I don't know. All I remember is, the day before he started middle school, in seventh grade, he said, 'If it wasn't against Jewish law, I'd kill myself.'"

"What?" Michael booms.

Caroline laughs. "You know drama runs in my family."

"But—"

"It worried me—of course—but I knew it was because he wasn't fitting in. I should have held him back, but he was so precocious. We used to joke that his first word was *hypothesis*, remember? And he was big for his age too. He was one of the youngest in his grade, but more mature than most of them, which maybe was the problem. He wasn't interested in the same things as his peers. I don't know. It was like, they'd be talking sports cars, and spy shows, and he could care less. He didn't pretend, and at a certain point he told me they gave him a lot of flak for not cursing. He also stood up for kids being bullied. There was this awful incident when he was in second or third grade and a kid he liked was being shoved around in the playground after school. He reported it to the bully's father, and you know what the guy did? He yelled at him. 'So, what are you, a great-big tattletale?'"

"Jerk," Michael says.

"It was horrible. Anyway, he was super smart and a voracious reader, and his interests kept changing, but he pursued everything full tilt. He's always been very passionate about stuff, which is a good thing. In fourth grade, he was taking lessons in C++, which was a computer program back in the day. In junior high, he became obsessed with rap music and graffiti. But he stopped liking school, and his grades were meh for such a bright kid."

"Meh?"

"Indifferent. He was an underachiever, but we knew he was learning. He just had different priorities. I remember one time he asked me to test him on a science chapter, how the human body functions. He hadn't memorized all the terms, but he really understood how the body works, I'll tell you that. I would venture to say he understood it better than most of his classmates. But it didn't matter. The test was on memorization."

"Sounds like you're making excuses for him," Michael says.

"He's quirky, that's all. Anyway, he's in a good place now. He did well in college, and he made some great friends there. So, we feel he's come out of the tunnel, but not without giving us plenty of heartburn."

"What sports does he like?"

She shrugs. "He'll humor Philip and watch football with him, but I don't think he watches on his own. I tried to interest him in your sports memorabilia."

"He doesn't like sports?"

"Shh. You'll wake my folks. He's not in your league when it comes to sports . . . sorry. He does love ice hockey. He was on the high school team and played intramural in college, and he's in an adult league now. Oh, and he likes mixed martial arts."

"Like what?"

"I'm not totally sure, lots of kicking."

Enough, she decides. She'd rather not tell him the rest. How Mark gave Philip such a hard time when he was a teenager, pouncing on everything he said. It came out of the blue, but he pushed Philip away, which was the only time she saw that husband in tears. Then there was the letter he wrote to both of them during his freshman year, a Dear John kind of piece:

First off, I want to thank you for making me feel like a well-loved kid, but it's time to acknowledge we are drifting.

He ended by stressing it was important to let them know he loved them *with all my heart, because you never know when the opportunity to say that will be revoked.*

It was his most morbid phase and her concerns intensified when he insisted on staying at school that summer. But then he fell in love with a girl named Anna and seemed much happier, although he got written up a few times for pot and underage drinking, and Philip had to retain a lawyer twice, and it was only near the end that he took his classes seriously.

"I was a really different person back then," he had said recently.

How many times had she dreamt of filling Michael in on the children's lives and her changing perspectives about parenting? But now that she has the chance, it is simply too hard. Too hard to convey someone's whole life, even a young man's, and, really, what was the point?

"Caroline, my head is spinning. You're all over the place."

"Well, I have a solution to that. Get out of my head! And you know what? I can't give you the full picture, sweetie. I'm sorry. Too much time has passed and you're right, you missed too much. But I'm glad you can see now that it hasn't been a picnic, because as his parent you should know that. Still, Mark's a hell of a guy and everything I told you is from before. None of it pertains to now." She hesitates, then takes his ghostly hand. "You must get permission to meet him. Plus, all your favorite food."

"I know, I know. And what about the baby? I'd love to see her too. We've barely talked about her. Is *she* athletic at least?"

"She's much more competitive than Mark. She was great at lacrosse."

Michael tears up again. "I can't believe I missed their games. I would have coached them. I can't believe I missed it all."

"Oh, and Michael, your dad will be here. It would be so great if you could attend. I know you want to see him."

"My dad's coming? Here?"

"Yes, here. We always have him at Thanksgiving. Isabel used to come too, of course."

"I had no idea," he says. More tears. "That's great of you, Caroline. Really. *And* your husband."

That's what he says, but now he looks troubled, deep in thought. He was close to his dad, so it can't be that. Besides, Spencer's so easy. He grew up in London before World War II and has retained his English accent and dignified air. The ghosts' visit might be even more overwhelming to Michael than to her, Caroline realizes.

She sighs. "I hope Julie comes," she says. "I really need to fill you in on her, too. I'm afraid she's gotten more and more difficult. She's still in the tunnel, from what we can tell. I don't—"

Bernice sings out:

Children can only grow

From something you love

To something you lose . . .

"Caroline, if my father's coming, I have to tell you something right now," Michael says.

"*Into the Woods*," Bernice exclaims.

"She awakens! Hel-lo, Dolly," Caroline calls to the other side of the room.

"Nope, *Into the Woods*."

As they walk toward her parents, she trips over a mound of papers that weren't there before. In fact, most of her discrete piles have been disturbed and the attic floor is blanketed with papers, documents, magazines, clothing, photos, books, framed baseball cards, and other sports artifacts from Michael's extensive collection. Not only are the deceased's possessions no longer relegated to columns of stacked and sealed boxes—there's been a complete invasion!

"Oh my God, Michael, enough already. You've ruined everything."

"Disturbing your sacred space? This stuff looks like it's been in a dusty crypt, sealed for eternity."

"Too bad. Stop it!"

"Stop what?"

"Stop going through my stuff. I know it was messy before, but now it looks like a hurricane came through."

"First off, as you said earlier, it's our stuff. And, as I've told you, I'm looking for something."

"What is it?"

That cagey smile again. "I can't tell you yet. It's a surprise."

"I hate surprises. Your deaths were a surprise."

"This is a good surprise, possibly a great one, Caroline. Hopefully you just have to wait a little longer—and you have to trust me."

"A man on a mission," Bernice says.

"It's just that I had a system going," Caroline protests.

"A mission of madness," Norman says, rousing from the dead. Bernice sings:

We disappoint,

We leave a mess,

We die but we don't . . .

"Sondheim?" Caroline asks.

Her mother nods. "Yes. *Into the Woods.* You remember. I'm impressed."

Bernice had been an aspiring singer, la, la, la. Caroline feels she can use *la, la, la*—sister to *blah, blah, blah*—instead of telling her mom's full story because her mother has changed it so many times. In one iteration, Bernice, in her early twenties—and a mere five-foot-two—was working for the Ford Modeling Agency when she was asked to cut a demo and offered a recording contract; in another, she was invited to audition for the local news anchor spot. Whatever happened, it was right when she became pregnant again and Norman allegedly dissuaded her from a glamorous career path because she would soon have two young children to raise. "I could have been a contender," she liked to say. Shortly before her death, Bernice told Caroline, for the first time, that she had sung at a Civil Rights benefit concert in Peekskill, New York, alongside Paul Robeson.

"You have to laugh about it, Caroline. What's the matter with you?" Michael ghost asks. "Where's your sense of humor? You seem distressed. We thought you'd be so happy to have us back."

"I am. I really am. I'm sorry. It's just, I'm overcome. I mean, the stuff about Dad, Norman." Her eyes fill, but then she grows angry. "And, I don't know, now that we're face to face again, I guess I'm still mad at you for crashing the family car and leaving me, even though I've made something of my life, I really have. And, also, no one's asked me about my writing."

"He was fixing my seatbelt," Bernice says. "I didn't have it on right, couldn't get the darn thing snapped."

"I was?" Michael asks.

"Yes, you were trying to help me, that's why you took your eyes off the road."

"I don't think that's true."

"Yes, you were. But it was my fault. I was being insistent."

"Wow," Norman says.

"Unbelievable," Caroline adds.

"So how *is* your writing going, darling?" Norman asks. "*Are* you still writing, Caroline?"

"Well, I haven't exactly taken the world by storm."

"We know nothing about that," Bernice says.

"We'd like to know," Michael says.

"Yeah. And don't be so hard on yourself. You're really talented," Bernice says.

"Okay, let's see. Since you all died, I've published three novels, the first with a Ballantine imprint that was reprinted in London, the others with smaller presses, but good ones. There aren't too many options these days because so many people are writing—you wouldn't believe how many, Michael—and mainstream opportunities for fiction are shrinking, blah, blah, blah."

"Still, three novels, that's great," her dad says.

"There are tons of copies in that storage closet if you get curious. Help yourself."

"What about now? Are you working on something now?" Michael asks.

"Yeah, sort of. Not every day. I've kind of lost my sense of urgency."

"You're more mature."

"Thanks, Michael."

"What's your latest book about?" he asks.

Caroline grins. "Oh, this sixty-year-old writer who's still struggling to deal with a profound tragedy from her past."

"You're kidding, right?"

Caroline shrugs. "I'm thinking maybe she'll be visited by ghosts."

"Have I ever told you about the time my father schlepped me and your grandmother all over the country looking for a new location for his paper-box factory?" Bernice asks.

Caroline sighs.

"I was about seven," Bernice continues, "and I remember we stayed at this really fancy hotel in Dallas, and my father bought me this nifty cowgirl outfit with a suede vest, horsehair skirt, hat, boots, the whole shebang. This tall man came up to us in the lobby and scooped me up just like that. He twirled me high in the air and said, 'Now isn't this the cutest little cowgirl ever.' He had a real Texas twang and he spoke to my dad for several minutes. When he left, I said, 'Daddy, who was that?'"

"And he said, 'The Lone Ranger,'" Caroline says.

"No, dear. He said it was Lyndon Johnson."

So, okay, besides the fact that Caroline has never heard this story before, it doesn't hold up. Would Popup know Lyndon Johnson by sight in 1944, when Bernice was seven?

"He *was* in Congress by then, but who knows," Michael says. "I'll tell you one thing though: It's pointless to challenge her. You're not going to dissuade her of this memory."

"She's the real fiction writer."

"Well, who's to say it didn't happen?" Michael asks.

"Yeah, who's to say, Caroline?" Bernice interjects.

"By the way, do you still scribble all night long?" Michael asks.

"Not as much."

"You're older now."

"As you keep reminding me."

"It's a good thing. You're lucky to grow old on earth."

"I know," Caroline says. "But it has its hard parts too."

Bernice sings a different tune:

A little grumpy

A little cranky

A little crabby . . .

"I don't think you've got those words right. *Pajama Game,* Mom?" Caroline asks. Her mom has such a pretty voice, although it's deeper and throatier than she remembers. Older.

"Hmm. You know, I can't remember where that's from, but let me tell you, dear, getting old sucks. It's not the fun part of the movie. As me ole dad used to say, 'My get up and go, got up and went.'"

"Have you seen Popup in heaven?" Caroline asks.

"Just a few glimpses because, as mentioned previously, we haven't quite made it to heaven yet, though we should have. We've waited long enough. We're worn out, pooped. You'll see someday. You have no energy, no stamina. You don't feel particularly great. Your mind's like a sieve. You see how much we nap, for God's sake! It's unabashedly dreadful."

Yup, this is the mom she knows and loves. Caroline is plenty aware of the downsides of aging, but she would never saddle her kids by telling them it was unabashedly dreadful. For her children, she tries to be brave and face things gracefully, keeping her anxieties to herself as much as possible. She believes parents should present themselves as fearless leaders; over time, kids manufacture plenty of dread on their own.

But Bernice seemed to lack that parental instinct. Flying was a prime example. Caroline would be readying to leave on a trip and Bernice would drone on and on: "Hope you're okay. Hope your flight's not a nightmare, like when I flew to Buffalo. That was the worst. People lurching all over the place. The stewardess bumped her head and passed out . . ."

"Mom, please, I'm trying to stay in a Zen place about it," Caroline would say.

But her mom never held back about the things that frightened her: flying, illness, getting shots, having procedures . . . getting old.

"How do you work this contraption? I've heard it has a stock market page." Norman to the rescue. He is waving Caroline's laptop in the air.

"Careful! Hey, where'd you get that? I was looking for it."

"What is it?"

"It's a computer, Dad. You had one. Don't you remember?"

"That was gigantic! It looked like an air conditioner."

Caroline laughs. "Yeah, they've really changed. This one's called a laptop." She takes it from her father and turns to Michael. "Have you been inspecting this too?"

"I tried. We couldn't turn it on," he says. "Why does it matter? Are you keeping secrets, Caroline?"

"Not secrets, exactly, but everything is on it. My whole life."

He looks skeptical. "Why do you keep it in the attic?"

"I don't. I brought it up here to catalogue stuff, so I can tell everyone where everything is. I'm old enough that I forgot I did that. I've been packing and repacking boxes these days because someday we're going to move."

"You'd sell the house?"

"We don't have immediate plans, but some day. Don't look crushed. It's good to purge now and a change might be good."

"You're keeping something from me," he says, trying to access her thoughts while she tries to think about anything but their moving plans: *red, green, blue, yellow, violet, teal. . .*

"You're planning to move soon," Michael says. "That's why everything's so pulled together downstairs. All the clutter's in the attic."

Mark had given her permission to clean out his bedroom so she could stage it as a guest room. She promised not to read anything and didn't think too much about it when she found some condom wrappers and beer caps in his desk drawers, although why would you hold onto condom wrappers? He has his first apartment with two friends, who also came back to the area after college. "You can toss it all," he had said. "I haven't needed it up till now, so I can't imagine I'll need it later."

"But you're only twenty-three," Caroline pushed back.

"You won't find much in my room," Julie had said when she finally addressed the matter via email. "Maybe since you save everything, I throw everything out."

Caroline has held off tackling Julie's room, but from Mark's she kept diplomas and articles he'd written for the high school paper, as well as a smattering of stories and drawings from when he was little. And his POGS and Slammers. He had loved those.

Oh yes, and his swimming certificates and essays. As with Michael's box, Mark might one day want to revisit his, or his wife might, who knows.

"Yikes," Michael says, covering his ears. "Yikes! So much noise in that head of yours."

"Then, for the umpteenth time, stop listening in!"

"From what I can tell, you've kept every piece of paper Mark deigned to touch."

"That gigantic computer?" Norman says. "All I ever used it for was that mail thingy, which I found tedious."

"Email, Dad. Would you like to check something out now, the stock market?"

"Speaking of losing things, has anyone seen my glasses?" Bernice asks.

"I assumed everyone's vision was twenty-twenty in heaven," Caroline says.

"Hah. I need glasses all the time now. My eyes are getting worse and worse."

"Can you see an optometrist up there?"

Bernice laughs. "Fat chance. But there's lots of glasses lying around. You take the ones that are closest to what you need."

Caroline's cell phone vibrates, and she glances at Philip's text. *Come down.* All eyes are on her. "Philip wants me downstairs."

"And that's how he summons you? He doesn't have the courtesy to come up here?" Bernice asks.

"Mom! I told her he can't. We can't meet him yet," Michael says, then to Caroline. "Yes, I call her *Mom.* It's easier. So, what is that? A walkie talkie?"

"Hey, remember those Dixie cups with strings coming out of them you and Bobby used to scream into?" Norman asks.

"It's a portable phone. And you can use it anywhere you go, even abroad."

"Whoa," the three ghosts say.

"And this device is even neater," Caroline says as she lifts the cover of her laptop and it chimes.

"Ah!" says her ghostly chorus.

"Could you check on some Wang stock for me, darling?" Norman asks. "I had that, I believe."

Her father had been a cautious man and not much of an investor. When he died, he'd had some bonds and a little bit of stock, but mostly he'd had savings accounts—five or six of them because he used to open new ones to get a free toaster or iron.

"I actually learned word processing on a Wang," Caroline says. "But they're long gone, I believe. I can tell you what happened to it." She types *Wang computers* as the others look over her shoulder. "Let's see." She reads directly from Wikipedia: "Founded in 1951. At its peak in the 1980s, Wang Laboratories had annual revenues of three billion and employed over 33,000 people. Filed for bankruptcy in August 1992." Caroline looks up. "So, a little before you died, Dad. You must have forgotten."

"Gracious, how did you do that?" Norman asks.

"The internet. Do you remember it? You can search anything you want." She exits from Wikipedia and shows them how to do a Google search. "Most people have Apples now—these laptops called Macs. And this is an Apple cell phone. There are Apple watches too. Apple's pretty much taken over."

"Apple!" Michael says.

"What?"

He looks delighted. "I just love the name."

"It was our time, that's why we died," Bernice says. "We were meant to live in a simpler era."

"That's preposterous—it wasn't your time," Caroline says.

"It was."

"Oh, come on, Mom. Why do you say that? I hate when people say things like that."

"We didn't think it at the time, but since it happened, it makes sense. So, we understand, we get it now. It's a good thing. Right, guys?"

Norman nods.

"It's true," Michael says. "There really is a bigger plan."

"Oh God, don't say that. You're freaking me out," Caroline says.

"Why?" Michael asks.

"I don't know—I just hate this kind of shit, especially since you keep saying you can't explain it. Can you? Can you even explain why you all just said what you did?"

They shake their heads no.

"It's too hard to explain," Bernice says.

"You're really going to sell the house?" Michael says, changing the subject.

"If we have the guts to follow through. I think it will be good for us."

"Do you go to The River Cafe with Philip?" he asks, dour again. It had been one of their favorite restaurants, a few towns over in a converted mill.

Caroline shakes her head no. "That's been closed for—"

A bang makes them all turn toward the stairs.

"I have to go," Caroline says.

The attic steps drop to the ground.

"No, no, wait," Michael says. "Your mom mentioned I had a surprise. I actually have two secrets—um, surprises—for you. One should make you quite happy, the other not so much."

"Well, that's unnerving. How unhappy will the bad one make me? Maybe start with that."

He opens his mouth, but someone else speaks.

"Caroline?" It's Jean, her best friend. "Caroline? You up there?" Jean rattled the base of the steps and shouted in sing-song, "Oh Car-o-line. It's Thanksgiving, remember? I'm coming up!"

"No, no, Jean. The steps are treacherous. Stay there! Don't come any closer. I'm coming down."

"What's up there—state secrets?" Jean asked.

Caroline waves goodbye to her threesome.

"Can you leave the laptop-thingy, please?" Michael says.

"Why?"

"We want to learn things. We're on a fact-finding mission."

"My guests are here, but I love you guys," she whispers as she heads to the stairs. "I've loved you this entire time."

"The guests are here? My father too?" she hears Michael ask. "Yikes. Wait! Caroline. WAIT. I have to tell you my first secret now!"

But this time it is she who vanishes.

"Cripes!"

◉ ◉ ◉

"Why are you so winded?" Jean asked after hugging her in the second-floor hallway. "Why is it so cold up here?"

"It's cold? I didn't realize. I'll turn the heat up. You know me, running up and down all the time, hard at work." She yanked her friend over to the front hall stairs, thinking Jean looked like a healthcare coordinator, with her crisp white turtleneck and long, flowing sweater. "I'm so glad you and Scott could come this year. What do you hear from Jeff?"

"He's decided to stay in Japan another year. He loves it there and it's great training for him, and he's met all kinds of people, so he's happy. We're going over in the spring, finally."

"Awesome," Caroline said. But that was another reason she felt grateful to have two kids, unlike Jean who just had Jeff. Once they were eighteen, it was likely one of them would be far away or hard to contact, and she liked having at least one in the vicinity. "Hey, come with me. I need your help with the appies."

A crashing sound came from the attic, followed by Michael's maniacal laugh, which she'd always found so unsettling, but had somehow managed to forget about all these years. She hadn't missed his temper and short fuse, and she had hated this laugh, which she used to hear even when he was at the opposite end of the house. It was a tormented laugh, loud and piercing. "Why does it bother you?" Michael would say. "I'm just pissed at myself."

"What was that?" Jean asked.

"What?"

"That thud. Is someone up there?"

"You mean besides me? It had to be a stack of boxes. They topple over sometimes."

"Boxes?" Jean said.

Her friend didn't seem to buy it—but Jean had merely heard a thud, not Michael's crazed laugh.

When they reached the first floor, Jupiter bounded up to them, crossing two rooms in five seconds and almost knocking Caroline down. Caroline bent over and let the dog lick her cheek over and over as Jupiter's long tail banged back and forth into Jean's thigh. "This is why I don't wear blush," she said to her friend.

"No greater love," Jean said.

"She misses me. I've been a bit AWOL."

Jupiter was really Julie's dog. When their old dog Jack died, Mark was so heartbroken that he made Caroline promise she wouldn't get another dog until he went to college. As soon as Mark left, Julie begged for a puppy. But now Julie was gone too, so Jupiter and Caroline were joined at the hip.

She spied Philip's briefcase, which he always stowed by the dining room credenza. She had asked him to take it to the bedroom for this occasion, but he must have forgotten. He was very attached to his briefcase, shouldering it to work every day even though, with rare exception, all it conveyed was *The New York Times*. He used to keep an i-Pad in it, but it no longer worked, so she didn't understand why he still had to lug his briefcase back and forth. It weighed him down. As a writer, she recognized a symbol when she saw one.

"Why does it bother you? It doesn't bother me," he said when she got after him about it.

Philip was someone who might die wishing he'd spent more time at the office, but generally he came home to her instead. He had his tussles with clients and cases, but he enjoyed other lawyers and the endless strategizing. He had hinted things weren't going so well right now, but that it was premature to discuss. Fortunately, she had lots of other stuff to distract her.

"It smells great in here," Jean said in the kitchen. "But Caroline, if you want me to help, I need direction. You seem super distracted."

"Things have been crazy lately."

"Everything all right?"

"Yeah, I guess. Yeah, everything's fine, amazing in some ways. I'd love to expand, but I'm having one of my godawful headaches."

"I'm sorry. Sit down. You can direct from your chair. Can I get you some aspirin?"

"I already took some. I'll be fine soon."

You had to love Jean. She had been such a great friend since they met in a neighborhood playgroup when their sons, both first children, were infants. Mark and Jeff stayed best friends for the first few years of elementary school, but grew apart after that; nevertheless, Jean and Caroline grew closer. Jean provided a range of support, from leaving encouraging cards in Caroline's mailbox to storing candy supplies in Jean's basement—Caroline couldn't resist post-holiday sales—and meting them out on request.

"I'm so happy you're here," Caroline said now.

"We are too. What's this peculiar thing?" Jean was fingering the large wreath Caroline had assembled as a centerpiece for the Thanksgiving table. Besides the pinecones and ferns, old letters, and yellowed paperback pages, it now held faded baby socks, smudged Troll dolls, little plastic cavemen and dinosaurs from the kids' diorama supply box, and a trove of creased baseball cards.

"It's creepy, but kind of intriguing," Jean said.

"Very diplomatic, Aunt Jean. How ya doing?" Mark gave Jean a hug before turning to Caroline, "We'll revisit my plan later, Mom?"

"What plan?" Jean asked.

"Didn't Mark get tall?" Caroline asked.

"Mom!" He started to walk away, then stopped. "I'm sure she'll explain it to you. And I'm counting on your support, Aunt Jean."

"So handsome!" Jean said. "What's that cheesy smell?"

"Oh my God, the appetizers!" Caroline opened the oven.

CHAPTER EIGHT

Here we go. Low fat, whole wheat green tea.
—fortune cookie

"S issy!" Mark said at the front door. "You made it. Fantastic." He reentered the living room with his little sister directly behind him, like they were speed skating and she was catching his draft. "Hey guys, look—Julie came!"

The frenetic reaching around for various hors d'oeuvres amidst various strains of conversation stopped and those seated opposite each other on two large crescent-shaped couches looked up to see a young woman with a slight physique emerge from behind her brother. As she fidgeted, a bunch of keys jangled on a chain hooked to the belt loop of her jeans, like she was the super of a large building. A few additional silver chains hung in circles down the side of her pants. On her neck was a multi-colored tattoo of an anchor with a red rose wrapped around it.

Subtle, Caroline thought. *And why no overnight bag?*

Julie's shiny jet-black hair was parted on the right so that the bulk of it flowed down the left side of her head and a braid ran from the front of the part down the back of her head. The braid was pink! Then Caroline saw a small ring pierced into the skin above Julie's right eyebrow. *Ouch!* She clenched her teeth and—she couldn't help it—started to worry.

"Hey everyone," Julie said. "I'm going by Jocelyn now."

Caroline shook her head several times in pleasant assent. "Okay, that's fine. Why Jocelyn?"

"It means *loving.* Some people say it means *joy.*"

"Both good," Caroline said. She placed her cracker of salmon pâté on the edge of the cocktail table so she could hug her daughter.

"Right behind you," Philip said.

It was only then, when Jocelyn turned toward her father, that Carolyn noticed what she had done to the other side of her head, which was shaved close, a buzz cut with a second anchor etched in it.

Obviously searching for roots, Caroline thought.

"It's a hair tattoo," Jocelyn said. "The anchor. Isn't it neat?"

Philip took Jocelyn into his arms. "Great to see you again, kiddo."

"Yeah, I feel good, a whole lot better," she said. "I think I've figured some things out."

"That's great," Caroline said, continuing to worry. Philip said it was her default mode, but she couldn't help worrying about her kids. Early on, she thought they would never learn to talk, then she was sure they'd be the only kids who never toilet trained—or couldn't learn to shower by themselves. Her worries grew bigger as the kids grew older and went through their phases. And it did seem that her kids went through more phases than most. Mark had an annoying macho phase at the start of college when he put on fifty pounds, mostly muscle, with the copious use of protein powder and non-stop weightlifting. For most of high school, Julie only wore black, so this latest presentation was perhaps an upgrade from that, although it just seemed her kids took things to the extreme. And try as Caroline might, she couldn't blame that on Philip's genes. Michael's, perhaps.

Jocelyn smiled, squeezing both parents' hands before stepping back. "I know you think I'm strange."

"We didn't say anything," Caroline said.

"You've always been strange," Philip said, then whispered, "It's why you fit in here."

"That's some belt you've got," Mark said.

Jocelyn wore a thick leather belt with assorted implements tucked into it, including a penknife, money pouch, and small hammer.

"Why do you need a flashlight?" he asked. "Did you join the fire department?"

"Funny. You can't be too prepared," she said.

"We're so glad you're here, Jule—ah, Jocelyn. We've missed you."

"Thanks, Mom."

"Hey, Jocelyn, great to see you," Jean said, standing and yanking her husband, Scott, along with her.

Mark pulled Caroline aside. "This is nothing to worry about, Mom. The sidecut's very trendy right now."

"Hel-lo, Julie," Scott said, a bit too loudly and with exaggerated glee. When he felt awkward, he did things with gusto. Forget about the dance floor.

"Not Julie—Jocelyn," Jean corrected. "I know your parents are really happy you made it today. We are, too. It's been a long time, right?"

"Yeah. But we have an arrangement, so it's all good. I've put myself in a kind of long time-out. It's helped and I'm sure they've carried on just fine without me. You know I've always been the outlier in this family."

⊙ ⊙ ⊙

Two days after Mark's fourth birthday, on a gray and drizzly early October day, Caroline dropped her son at pre-K and ran into the Westside Mall to meditate with the aid of a large cappuccino.

Since she took sips of coffee while she sat upright and still, it wasn't strictly meditating, but she concentrated her breaths, and it served as time out of time, like when you're alone on a train, a chance to relax and let waves of tension pass through you and exit the other side. It helped, so good enough, even if it was the slowest fifteen minutes of her life . . . every time!

Looking back, she can't imagine why she was so tense at that time, just some hard-wired predisposition to thinking the Sword of Damocles dangled overhead.

Energized by all the caffeine, she climbed two sets of stairs to the third floor to use the women's room before heading out. The lounge appeared to be empty, but as she sat in one of the stalls, Caroline heard a rustling from the wall beside her, followed by soft moans. Washing her hands in front of the large mirrors, she heard the sounds again. They were coming from the stall directly behind her—its door ajar. Inside, she found a tiny baby strapped in an infant seat mounted on the wall of the stall, a place to stow your baby while you used the facilities. *Koala Kare Child Protection Safety Seat*, it said. The baby was slouched down in it, way too small for the apparatus, but secure because the belt around its middle was fastened tight.

The baby was listless, not exactly asleep, but dazed. Or maybe it *was* sleeping, not in the angelic way babies usually sleep, but with an expression of despair, its eyes and miniature hands squeezed tight, its lips pursed in pain.

Caroline stood halfway in and halfway out of the stall. A stranger entered the lounge, a woman her mother's age. She eyed Caroline suspiciously.

Caroline returned to the stall, shutting the door behind her. *Who stands up for this child?* she thought.

The baby gave a cry.

Who is with this child?

As soon as the older woman had locked herself in a stall,

Caroline rescued the infant from the seat and grasped her to her chest. The baby cried in earnest then, although still not loudly because she was so weak. Her faded pink pajamas were damp and her diaper heavy. Caroline headed to the mall's management office in the basement, near Macy's. She knew where it was because she had left her wallet in the food court a week earlier and recovered it from there. By the time she arrived, the baby's shrieks had subsided. She was now trying to suckle, wetting Caroline's blouse.

"Someone left this baby in the ladies' room," Caroline said. "In a stall."

"Dear goodness," the management woman said. "How horrible. I'll call the police. And an ambulance."

Caroline sat with the baby and waited. The infant had conked out in her arms.

The medics took the baby from her, and the police took down her account right there in the mall, after which Caroline added, "I have to talk to my husband, but if no one claims this baby, I want to know. I'm interested."

It just came out, like when she had asked Philip to marry her—she just blurted it out. She had held the tiny girl for fifteen minutes, but there wasn't a second when she thought she wouldn't keep this baby.

"Sure lady," the policeman said, repeating her telephone number. "You'll be receiving a follow-up call about the incident. Tell them."

"Incident?" Caroline asked. "You mean, tragedy!"

The policeman stood there.

Baby Julie spent weeks in the hospital before Caroline and Michael were able to bring her home, and then it was a fostering arrangement at first, meaning if the real mother—or father—came forward, they would have to give her up.

The wait was interminable. Caroline read about people who

had been in their position and lost the right to adopt at the last minute. They were cautioned not to become too attached. But, of course, they became attached immediately.

◎ ◎ ◎

"Still a no-meatarian?" Mark asked his sibling.

"Vegetarians, we're called."

"It's not like you eat a ton of vegetables, though—just no meat?"

"Mostly I eat Styrofoam," Jocelyn said.

"We've missed you," Philip said, kissing her cheek. She smiled and seemed happy enough to be here. He felt relieved. He would leave it to Caroline to figure out the whole Julie-slash-Jocelyn thing at the appropriate time. "Have you said hello to your grandfather?" he asked.

This was Michael's father, Spencer, the only grandparent left. Philip's mother had died when he was thirteen, and his father when he was thirty. He was drawn to the elderly, but for years things remained awkward between Michael's parents and him. They had wanted to embrace him, but they were still grieving and here he was interloping on their son's family. Also, although Caroline disagreed, Philip knew it bothered Michael's mother, Isabel, that he wasn't Jewish. Still, he had to give them credit. They adored their son's children, now Philip's, and slowly they warmed to his stepping in.

"Jocelyn," Spencer said. "Well, aren't you always full of surprises."

He really dresses like an Englishman, Jocelyn thought, in his Harris Tweed jacket with dark brown elbow patches that looked like it was fifty years old, from a time when he might have aspired to do graduate work in Irish literature at Trinity Dublin. Maybe it was the pale-blue ascot. To the manor born.

"Howdy, Grandpa. Great to see you," she said, taking his hand for a moment. It had a *plethora*—a word deployed in her college-admissions essay—of bulging green-blue veins and his skin was very thin. That made her sad. "Whacha been up to, gramps?"

"Grandpa to you, dear. I've been up to nothing. 'Tis a problem."

"You must be doing something?"

"Oh, yes, still at it."

"You're still working? In the City?"

"Not officially. Just when they're desperate at my old firm. Not often, truth be told. And up to nothing otherwise. Thank goodness for Thanksgiving, if that's not redundant." Spencer reached toward the cocktail table, waving his veiny hand back and forth over the assortment of appetizers before stuffing a stuffed mushroom in his mouth—if that wasn't redundant. "I'm lucky this family keeps me in its fold. I've gotten a little quirky myself since my dear Isabel's death. I'm old! Even so, may I ask what's prompted your stylish flourishes?"

"I'm getting old too," Jocelyn said.

"Hah. I have socks older than you."

"I miss Grandma Isabel."

"Yes," he said, looking up. "It'd be lovely to see her, wouldn't it? I've been praying for that."

"You mean praying to die?"

Spencer shrugged his tweedy shoulders.

"Jocelyn, can you help us?" Jean asked, tugging on her sleeve. "Excuse us, Spencer. Reinforcements needed in the kitchen."

"Do you think my grandpa's okay?" Jocelyn asked Jean once they were out of earshot. "I mean, he's really old now, and he seems glum."

"I think he's pretty sharp. He told me he still writes poetry. He's kind of cool actually."

Jocelyn laughed. "Yeah, kind of. Mom, it smells incredible in here!"

"Ah, you're just saying that."

"No, really."

Caroline yanked the oven shelf out to baste the giant bird.

"Should I dress the salad?" Jocelyn asked.

Caroline hugged Jocelyn, rubbing the anchor stamped into the right, creative side of her daughter's head. She didn't know what to make of her daughter's recent fashion decisions, and she couldn't stop wondering what Michael would think of it all. He had better not freak out. Having Julie in their life was something that had gone really well on the whole, and Caroline was grateful. Adoption was risky. She personally knew two couples whose adopted children had serious, seemingly lifelong, problems. One of them was a drug addict in prison.

Scott and Spencer entered. "Kitchens are great, right? Best place to hang," Scott said. He observed all the dishes everywhere. "This is seriously a lot to eat in the middle of the afternoon, Caroline. Why'd you call it so early?"

"Aren't you always hungry, Scott? I know I am, so why not start early instead of sitting around or pacing in our own homes waiting for it to be time to gather? It's like the airport. People like to wait until the last minute so they don't have to hang out at the airport too long, but it's not like it's so great waiting at home since the whole time you're worrying about when you should get to the airport. That's why I always go early."

"I don't spend the whole time worrying when I should get to the airport," Scott said.

"Whatever," Caroline said.

"You're looking round and lovely, Caroline," Spencer said, drifting into the kitchen.

"I'm not a turkey, Spencer, uh, Dad," she said. Isabel and Spencer had insisted she call them Mom and Dad, although to this day she found it hard. She already had a Mom and Dad, so to speak. "Julie, come with me," she said, then grunted at her daughter. "You know when I say Julie I really mean Jocelyn."

◉ ◉ ◉

"Who else are we waiting for? Mom?" Mark called out twenty minutes later. "Dad—where's Mom?"

Philip frowned. "Excuse me, Spencer . . . although I'd like to hear more about this. If I had to guess, Mark, she's in the attic."

But she wasn't in the attic. She was with Jocelyn in the basement searching for tonic water for Scott.

"What's with your finger?" Jocelyn asked. Caroline's index finger was covered with three blood-stained bandages.

"I've been cooking. I always bleed when I cook."

"You go too fast," Jocelyn said.

"Everyone's a critic."

"I bet there's some very old tonic in here," Jocelyn said, wandering away into the old walk-in pantry. When they were kids, she and Mark had loved playing in there because the shelves were packed with odd, but hearty, canned goods the family would never eat regularly, like lasagna soup and sirloin burger stew. Apparently, Nana Bernice, who died when Julie was a baby, had kept a similar stockpile during what she called the "duck and cover 1960s," when everyone feared a nuclear attack and you practiced hiding under your school desks—for whatever good that would do you. Jocelyn's mother had started stocking their pantry after 9/11.

If you were lucky enough to be home when an attack came, you would take refuge in your basement and eat stores of canned foods—cold, Jocelyn supposed. Two can openers preserved in their packaging hung prominently on hooks for the doomsday event. Keeping the pantry properly supplied was an exacting chore. Eventually, as the products reached their best-used-by dates, the family had to consume them, after which Jocelyn's mom dutifully replaced them with new cans that had expiration dates much farther out.

Even though it was a pantry, it had been designed with care because this was an old house, built at the turn of the twentieth century. The basement had once been a beauty, featuring a mahogany bar, banquette booths and tables, and a large mirror with an art deco maiden etched into it. Philip and Caroline had never entertained down there, giving Mark and Julie the run of the place instead. Despite a wide age range, the neighborhood kids all played in the basement together, and the maiden had a crack running from the top of her curly art deco locks, through the nipple of her left breast, to the bottom of her flexed toes, the result of an errant pitch. An enclosed padded booth by the bar was designed for projecting 35 mm film. It was a great hide-'n-seek spot, and when they were very small, Mark and Julie squeezed inside together and pretended they were on a picnic with their bowls of Froot Loops or Lucky Charms.

Together, they had pretty much trashed the place.

Julie had liked being Mark's little sister and he had watched out for her. He accepted her, no-holds-barred, even once it was revealed that she was adopted after being discarded in a public bathroom.

"Not discarded—discovered," her mom maintained.

Jocelyn returned from the pantry. "Canned goods, canned goods, everywhere, but not a tonic water in sight. Hey, Mom, know what I was just thinking about? Remember when we had a tent down here, and I made you come inside with me and listen to songs I liked?"

Caroline seemed pleased by the subject. "Yeah, on that little gizmo of yours."

Jocelyn laughed. "My MP3 player, and then my iPod nano."

"Seems like last year."

"Hardly! You were always rating them based on the lyrics, and I would try to tell you it wasn't all about the lyrics. Remember we used to argue about that?"

"I do. It's true, I'm very partial to lyrics," Caroline said.

Jocelyn smiled. "Yeah, but it was nice of you to listen because it wasn't your music—at all—and we did it a lot."

"I liked some of it. My memory is that your tastes were rather eclectic."

"I think you liked 'Panic! At the Disco.'"

"Yeah, that was a good song."

"It's a group, Mom! I know you didn't like the ones I showed you upstairs on our old computer, with explicit language."

"I'm your mother," Caroline said. "Why change your name by the way?"

"I like Jocelyn."

"It's a little long, no? Jo-ce-lyn?"

"No longer than Car-o-line."

"Touché. What about that thing near your eyebrow? It must hurt. Doesn't it catch on things?"

"It doesn't. And it doesn't hurt."

"How does it stay in there?"

"Mom! Don't touch. Why do you have to examine everything?"

"You're right, you're right." Caroline put her hands in her pockets and took a step back. *Well, please just don't get any more tattoos, especially visible ones*, she wanted to say, but caught herself. It would be the kiss of death, as Bernice liked to say, probably make her go right out and get another one. Better to act cool.

"So, have you decided what you're going to do next?" Caroline asked in a casual tone.

"I'm thinking a few more brow rings next to this one?"

"Jocelyn, you know what I mean—with your life?"

"Jeez, I bet my boyfriend you couldn't go ten minutes without asking me about plans. We haven't even eaten yet."

"It's at least twenty minutes. You have a boyfriend?"

She brightened. "I do. Uh, more on him later."

"Okay, but I do want to hear more."

Jocelyn gently punched Caroline's bicep. "Mom, I know you like to worry, but don't worry about me."

"How can you be so certain there's nothing seriously wrong?" Caroline had asked her neurologist a month ago.

"Because of your eyes, Caroline. If there were something serious, I'd be able to see irregularities in the rims around the cornea."

"I'm not going to die of a brain tumor?"

"No, I assure you—one hundred percent. It's your sinuses!"

She had jumped off the examining table, delighted by the definitiveness of his statement. When do they ever give you one hundred percent odds?

◉ ◉ ◉

"It's Bobby," Mark called out as he opened the front door.

"Uncle Bobby to you," Bobby said. "Hey, big guy." He shook his nephew's hand. "How's it going?"

"Great. I'm doing great."

"Awesome. You look great."

"Come in, come in—shut the door," Caroline said, rushing

toward them. "Hurry. It's freezing out there." She gave her brother a hug. "Two hours late, Bob?"

"Ninety minutes late, and sorry, sis. But two o'clock's awfully early for a dinner party, don't you think? Is anyone even hungry then?"

"Ugh. You're going to give me grief too? Besides, it's almost four. And it's Thanksgiving, not just any old dinner." Caroline laughed. "Also, what does hunger have to do with it? Come see." Hooking her arm in his, she led him to the dining room where the others had commenced an abundant meal. The table was crammed with large, colorful serving plates and bowls, all heaping. Caroline had never met a Thanksgiving dish she didn't like.

Bobby tossed his overcoat to Mark. "Wow, what a spread." He pulled out a chair. "Hi everyone. Deb sends her best, and apologies. She's not feeling well, so I left her in bed."

"Where's Jason?" Mark asked.

"I'm not sure. I know, I know, he should be here. Sorry." Bobby started to sit, then stopped, upright again. "By the way, you should check out the three dudes at the bottom of your front walk, the oddest-looking group. I didn't want to stare . . . but they're just standing there. Have you seen them? They look like they want to come in."

The doorbell rings.

The color drains from Caroline's face as she turns to her brother. "My God, no! Bob, did they look familiar to you?"

"They were huddled together, their heads down, so I couldn't really see their—"

She doesn't wait for her brother to finish, colliding into him in her rush to the door.

"We're here," someone says.

"How? How the hell'd you get here?" Caroline's voice is loud and suddenly an octave higher.

The dinner guests rise in unison and crowd into the foyer. At the front door, they see three souls: a late-middle-aged couple flanking a tall, dark, and handsome man, maybe forty.

"Good lord!" Philip says.

"Now everyone can see you?" Caroline shrieks at the trio.

"We got permission, sweetie. Finally. It just came down!" the younger man proclaims, pointing upward and grinning, although on closer examination his eyes are rimmed with red, as if he's recently been crying. "I'm as surprised and delighted as you, Caroline."

As Caroline falls to the ground in a faint, Mark manages to bend over and wedge his hands under her head before it slams on the floor. "Mom!"

"Honey!" Philip says.

The three appear to be locked together, gripping each other's hands as they step over Caroline and enter the hall. They are shivering, not wearing coats. In fact, they are wearing the most improbable outfits, old-fashioned and threadbare with nothing matching at all. The older man presses a few paperback books to his chest.

CHAPTER NINE

Fear drives you and makes you better.
—fortune cookie

W hen Caroline opens her eyes, she is lying on one of the living room couches and the first thing she sees are the *beatific* faces of her two grown children crouched over her. Hmm, beatific is perhaps the wrong word here as they look positively alarmed even as their faces glow—but they are thrilled to see their mother is alive. Or maybe their faces glow because they are young. Such beautiful skin. A shot of light streaks across the left side of Caroline's head, which throbs in 4/4 time—or is there a jazz ensemble nearby? Or is this heaven?

"Mom, what happened? Who are they?" Mark asks.

"You really scared us, Mom. There's some creepy-creepy looking people here," Jocelyn says in a tremulous voice.

Julie's here. Julie came. But she goes by Jocelyn now and she has a tattoo and a shaved head, and a piercing, and she looks frightened. Wait till she learns they are ghosts.

Julie had always been fearful—not unlike her mom—although brave enough to get a tattoo on her neck and a hole in her forehead. Luckily, Caroline is good in a crisis. She will rally and act like a triage nurse, reassuring her family and guests. She has risen to the task before, has always been great in emergencies, like when the kids needed stitches. *Help Jocelyn first,* she thinks. *What about Jean?*

Jean is calm, as is Scott; he's always laughing. So, they can wait for now. Philip she can count on. He will help Jocelyn. And Mark is brave. But BOBBY! And SPENCER! They are going to die when they see these visitors.

On cue, Philip walks in with her three ghosts respectfully trailing him: her mother, Michael in the middle this time, and Norman, who it turns out is not her real dad, although he certainly was the quintessential father. Did her mother really tell her that a dog bit his testicles? The ghosts are glued together and cautiously smiling. They look different now—more like the living. They plant themselves at the back of the room, lean in sync against the wall. The others stand clear of them. Michael is her parents' nursemaid, and whoever would have thought him up to that? Not that he wasn't loving and attentive as a dad, but in a roughhousing, all-fun-and-games sort of way. But he's so nice to her folks, and they aren't even his parents. She grasps her head. *Throb, throb, throb.*

"Honey! What the hell's going on?" Philip, her husband in the here-and-now, asks as their children recede, allowing him to inch next to her. Philip has been a better nursemaid to her than Michael ever was, although his expression can be hard to read, a litigator's poker face. Just now, she senses hostility as he yanks her up by her elbows to a sitting position.

"Ow," she says, pulling away so she can hold her head some more. She slumps into the cushions.

"You're killing me, honey. I really don't appreciate you doing that," Philip says.

"Doing what?"

"Fainting."

"It wasn't something I could control, Philip. It's not like I did it on purpose. Must be dehydrated."

He's just concerned—she can see it in his eyes. And he's almost as pale as the ghosts were earlier.

"What's wrong?" he says. "You scared me."

"My head hurts. You have to be nice to me."

"I'm sorry. I didn't mean to be rough, but, honey, we have a houseful of people, including three I don't think are supposed to be—"

"I'll get you a hot compress," her dear friend Jean calls out from somewhere.

"Jean, what's wrong? You look like you've seen a goblin," Jean's husband, Scott, says as he enters, laughing as always, squeezing Jupiter's leash up high. A five-year-old puppy, Jupiter strains to pull her handler nearer to the ghosts, but Scott is strong. He and Jean are in their mid-fifties, and they do P90X at six every morning.

Caroline turns Philip's head toward her. "I can't deal with everyone holus-bolus like this. You can see them, right?" she whispers.

"We all can, Caroline," he says. "And they look oddly familiar, but this can't possibly be right. Right?"

"Are they scary?"

"Not in the least. But how is this possi—"

"Shh," she says, putting her fingers over his lips, which he brushes away. "You might be right, I'll grant you that, but let's keep it a secret if we can. I don't think we can tell everyone the truth right now. I'm not even sure I'm allowed to."

"Allowed to? Who's calling the shots here?"

"They have lots of rules. I'll fill you in soon, I promise. I never expected them to come downstairs, honey."

"They were in the attic! I knew it. You were harboring them."

"Oh, hello there," she says to her father as he bends toward her, his head almost touching Philip's.

"Kids? Can you help me get something for your mom's head?" Jean calls out. "And we need to turn the heat up. It's suddenly so cold in here."

"Hello, darling one," Norman says.

Philip relinquishes the space a little but stays close. Along with Norman, he and Michael form a barrier around Caroline, shielding her from the others. Bernice is nowhere to be seen, which means the three ghosts are unbound again.

"So, you got permission," Caroline says to Norman.

"Finally, a stroke of luck. We've waited so long."

"Well, you look great. Better than before the accident, and much better than you looked upstairs." She wills herself upright to kiss her dad's cheek, which feels almost human, if still clammy. "In fact, how'd you do it? You've got some color now, no longer translucent. Seriously, much improved! Really handsome, Dad."

"I heard that," Philip says and Caroline winks at him.

Norman beams. "It's like coming out of anesthesia. I'm thinking clearer too. And thank you for continuing to call me Dad, darling. I *am* your dad, truly."

"My one and only," Caroline says. She stands gingerly, taking his damp hand for support, and whispers, "I love you" into his ear.

"That tickles!" Norman says. He holds up three of her novels. "May I have these?"

For the first time, Caroline smiles. "Of course. Please. Hey, Dad, your nose is straight now, perfectly straight. It wasn't before. You had that big bump."

"From fighting Marcus Altieri in high school."

"So, you always said. Whoa!" Caroline sinks back into the

couch. "I'm so dizzy. At any rate, it looks good, your nose. And your hair is salt and pepper again. And you're slimmer."

Michael pushes forward, jockeying for position in front of Norman and Philip so he can whisper in Caroline's ear.

Philip backs away, heads for the kitchen.

"It's the transformation, sweetie, our cover for the sake of the others. For your guests. As you know, we can be rather ghoulish, and our purpose is not to frighten people."

"Well, you certainly frightened me when you first arrived."

"Yeah, we're only permitted to outright shock one person, and that was you."

"Thanks."

"Our pleasure. So, we look good now, right?"

"You're shivering."

"Much colder here on earth, especially on the ground floor. Hot air rises, I guess. And bad weather's rolling in. I'm not dressed for it."

His short-sleeve madras shirt is thin from wear. Her mother at least has that lambswool vest and her father his tattered tennis sweater.

"I thought the cold air came with you. You couldn't change your clothes?" Caroline asks.

"Picky, picky," says Michael.

"Well, you have much better color all around. My dad looks wonderful, and you look changed too somehow. I can't quite put my finger on it." For one thing, he's as lean as a teenager and appears even younger than when he died at forty-two. But something else . . .

"I'm ripped," he says. Then he asks, "Don't you still want me, sweetie? Maybe we could slip away for a little cuddle."

"Yeah, sure. Uh, I can't do that."

"Why not?"

She laughs. "For starters, I get too hot."

"Hot is good."

"I mean literally hot. Anyway, I just can't."

Michael sticks his chest out. "Disguised and improved," he says proudly.

"Improved, but not so disguised. I don't think you'll fool anyone."

"Transformed!" Michael says. "We can't stay long, but while we're here—in those rare cases when we are granted permission to infiltrate—we are given the tools to appear as convincing humans, not mere *spirts*, which is the word they use for you after you die."

"Spirits?"

"No, spirts. That wasn't a verbal typo, Caroline."

"But you couldn't update your clothes? They're a little obvious."

"Yeah, we're not allowed to do that. Go figure. But I felt we needed some degree of disguise or all hell would break loose."

"But it's not enough. My dad's in a tuxedo!"

"Just his pants. He says they're super comfortable."

"Well, anyway, don't you want them to know who you are? Isn't that why you're here? Otherwise, what's the point of coming downstairs?"

"We will reveal ourselves, of course, but in time. I thought we could ease them in by not being fully recognizable."

"Then you should have pushed it more."

"Whatever, Caroline. Who cares! At a minimum we get to look our best, and it's the closest I'll get to playing God, that's for sure."

Finally sitting upright with a cold washcloth draped over her head, Caroline surveys the room. Her kids and guests stand way back—appropriately bewildered—while her mother mills around, introducing herself like a hostess at a fundraiser. Philip has returned, but remains at a distance.

Bernice is the most transformed. She is thinner than she ever was, even though that expressly goes against the rules she said govern them up there. Her hair is chestnut-colored and thicker, her cheekbones more pronounced. She is gorgeous, although she smells like a medicated heat patch for a sore back.

Water drips from the washcloth onto Caroline's gray wool pants.

Michael follows Caroline's gaze to her mother. "The transformation," he repeats.

"So, what's your plan?" Caroline asks.

Bobby approaches.

"Hey bro," Michael says and Caroline glares at him.

"Now you're being a tease," she says.

"Caroline. Caroline. Caro—," Bobby stammers.

"It's okay, Bobby," Caroline says.

"Mom, Dad, and Michael? What's going on?" Bobby pinches his former brother-in-law's forearm, but Michael doesn't react. "They're eidolons, right? I've read about this," Bobby says.

"It's not what you think, Bobby," Caroline says reflexively.

"Like hell it isn't. What are you going to tell me, they're look-alikes? If so, they're perfect!"

"Okay, it *is* what you think," she says. "Aren't they extraordinary?"

"We can eat too," Michael says. "Just today, and I must say it smells delicious."

Bobby's jaw drops.

More crazy rules from purgatory. It reminds her of the weird games Michael used to invent, idiosyncratic exceptions for ping pong, badminton, and HORSE, deviations that became even more elaborate and quirky when he was losing. He would switch to shooting the basketball left-handed so he could use that as the excuse. And he was a sullen loser. They'd had to ban Scrabble from the house.

Caroline stands, seizing Bobby's arm for support and maybe also to steady him. "Come with me, Bob."

She's tired and not entirely sure this isn't a dream after all.

"Hi. I'm Blanche," she hears her mom say to Philip, poking him in the back as she offers her other, now-corporeal hand. "So, so, so nice to meet you. Heard lots."

"No, you haven't!" Caroline says.

"Man-nay," Norman says to Philip, and they shake.

"Miguel," Michael says, chuckling, but keeping his hands by his side.

"Why are you guys using fake names? They already recognize you."

"Relax, Caroline."

"Okay, suit yourself, but this is ridiculous."

It reminds her of the time she and a college roommate were asked to join two older men for drinks at their table in a bar at the Plaza Hotel. Her roommate introduced herself using her middle name, Stacey.

"And what about you, miss," one of the men said to Caroline and her mind went blank. She couldn't think of any female names other than her own and her friend's, and maybe Bernice, but that wouldn't have been believable. After too long a pause, she said, "My name's Stacey too," causing her roommate to double over with laughter.

She must talk to the ones who don't recognize the ghosts: her kids, and Jean and Scott. But how can she explain?

"They grew up in the islands where they speak a kind of patois, I believe," Bernice explains to Philip. "Isn't that right guys?"

"Interesting," Philip says.

Spencer, who alone had stayed at the dining room table eating and drinking until a moment ago, enters with a look of both disbelief and rapture. He walks right up to his son and places his arm around his waist. "Mikey, is it really you?"

Michael lights up, but whispers, "Shh, it is, but I'm going with Miguel for now. Surprised?"

"Miguel? Got it. You bet I'm surprised."

Jean reaches Caroline with a new wet washcloth. She looks alarmed.

"Thanks, Jean, but I'm fine now," Caroline says. How can she explain?

"Do you know who these people are, Jean?" Bobby asks. "Can you guess?"

"They're from my grief group," Caroline tells Jean. "I invited them to Thanksgiving because they had nowhere else to go, and isn't that what the holiday's about: inclusivity? Speaking of which, the meal's halfway served, so I'd appreciate it if you could help me get everyone back to the dining room. Philip, would you get me some Tylenol, please—maybe three? And kids, can you reheat the dishes on the table so we can start again? Jean, come with me. Bobby and Spencer, can you entertain our guests? Where's Scott?"

Bobby feels Michael's arm around his shoulder.

Jean grabs Caroline's arm. "Scott took Jupiter back outside. She was frantic when you fainted. And she's totally weirded out by your visitors. They're not really from your grief group, Caroline, are they? You told me you stopped going years ago. And how is it they know everyone? Also, they look bizarre! They're *off*, more than off. Something's really off about them."

"Do you smell something burning?" Caroline asks.

"Tell me what's happening, Caroline! Why are these people

dressed like this? I mean, it's really maudlin if you sought them out. They're right out of that album you showed me, your first husband, your parents."

"Who's maudlin?" Bernice interrupts.

"It's sick, Car," Jean mumbles.

"Who's sick?" Bernice asks.

"Jean, listen. You're right, something weird's going on, well, not weird, fantastic. But will you play along with me until I can explain to the kids? Please?"

Scott joins them. "I hooked Jupiter to her tie-out chain. She's very entertained. Your backyard's like an aviary," he says.

"So, they're not people you picked up? They're what I think?" Caroline nods.

Jean's shoulders relax and she smiles broadly. "Then it's a miracle. But, Caroline, you need to tell the kids now."

"So, what are we waiting for? Let's eat!" Caroline says.

"Great," Bernice says. "I haven't eaten in a millennium."

"Jean, Scott—would you please sit with Blanche and Mannay? They won't bite, and I'm sure they can tell you some interesting stories."

"Why are their clothes so weird? That one guy's in tuxedo pants," Jocelyn says to Jean, her voice still shaky.

Norman spins around to face them, having somehow heard her from across the room. "We get to wear our favorite duds," he says.

"Your mom says they don't have a lot of money," Jean says, playing along for now.

◉ ◉ ◉

As the group files into the dining room, Caroline fixes her eyes on Michael, who is in the living room lingering over the console table covered with framed photos of different shapes and sizes.

He rubs his hand along the table's side. No doubt he remembers that piece, crafted of exotic wood from the Philippines, the only item of furniture from her first marriage that hadn't come from Ikea.

Michael studies each photo, checking the back for the date he knows Caroline has put there. Next, he scopes out the photos on the fireplace mantle.

His face is anguished. "All these pictures post-date us. How come?"

"That's not true. There are baby photos, lots of them. Don't you see them?"

"But none of *us* anywhere. Not one of me. Or your parents. It's so mean, Caroline. Why?"

"Because of the kids, Michael . . . *Miguel.*" She laughs painfully.

"You've suppressed the kids' memories of me. That's not how it's supposed to be. That's not right, Caroline. They're supposed to know about me." A puff of black smoke rises from his head and Caroline shivers. She checks if anyone else has seen—and there is Philip, standing at the room's entrance with his hands on his hips.

"Don't worry," Philip says. "At this point I'm incapable of being surprised. I mean, they look like something out of Madame Tussauds, but if I'm not mistaken, they also look precisely like your parents and first husband, no?"

"You know I can hear you, right?" Michael says.

"Can you believe it, honey? Did you ever think you'd see something like this?"

"Why were you hiding them?" Philip asks.

"I didn't want to. It's just they needed to get permission first, to come downstairs."

"Jews celebrate the dead," Michael says. "Remember what

they say in shul—every week, Caroline? 'We remember them. For as long as we live, they too will live . . . . To be loved is to live forever in someone's heart,' etc."

"That last bit's not from temple. You got that from a greeting card or something."

"Who cares? You know what I mean, Caroline."

Mark and Jocelyn join Philip in the doorway. Philip coughs to alert his wife, but she can see the kids are beginning to understand.

"Let's not get melodramatic, Michael," Caroline says. "Your memory *is* a blessing, I assure you—then, now, and always. And trust me, I've carried you around with me, all three of you, all these years. Never for a moment have you been forgotten." She pauses. "I've told them about you, lots of things, but I guess I kept the photos hidden to protect them, especially Mark."

An image fills her head of her four-year-old son clutching Michael's favorite baseball cap, blue and orange—the Mets—as he wandered around the house searching for his father.

"He was old enough to remember you, Michael. And it was horrendous enough for a small boy to lose his dad. He didn't also have to grieve his grandparents, whom he had seen much less and could forget more easily. At least that was my logic— help Mark forget."

"And yourself."

"Well, I told you, it hasn't been easy. Maybe if I'd known you could come back—if you'd come back sooner. Besides, I've kept the photos, all of them. You've seen what I have up there."

What part did Philip play in protecting Caroline and the kids by discouraging her from visiting the past too often? Wasn't it partly for him that she'd stored the photographs away? Philip tried not to stifle her, but his face looked stricken at the mere mention of Michael's name. Still, to be fair, it was mainly for herself and Mark, and despite her penchant for self-recrimination, she did not feel badly. Removing their photographs was an essential coping mechanism.

"By the way, he's too old for you," Michael says, indicating Philip.

"You know I can hear *you*," Philip says, pointing his finger at Michael.

"Guys, really? You're basically the same age . . . if you use your real age, Michael," Caroline says. "And he's a lot more mature"—she points to Philip—"usually. Look, we can't continue this conversation now. It's rude. We have guests and the jig is up."

"I would have liked having their photos around," Mark says to his mother. "Maybe you shouldn't have hidden everything. Might have brought them sooner."

Michael shakes his head in agreement, then throws up his hands. "Maybe."

"But you'd shown me some, Mom. I knew it was them," Mark says.

"I can't believe it's you," Michael says, looking his son up and down.

"Same," Mark says.

Michael extends his hand to shake, but Mark wraps his arms around the visitor.

◉ ◉ ◉

They are on the same page now with everyone having absorbed the reality of the three unearthly visitors quite well. Jocelyn was the most alarmed by the phenomenon of a visit from ghosts, but Philip has managed to settle her down. Though Jocelyn tends to share more intimate matters with Caroline, Philip has always been the one to calm her. Jocelyn claims it's his predilection for talking about things in universal terms.

Plus, Jocelyn is intrigued by all the rules the ghosts are sharing about the phase of heaven they're in now.

"It sounds like a weird existence," Mark says. "In some ways, it doesn't sound so different from here. No one knows what's going on . . . everything is confusing."

Caroline sits at the head of the long Thanksgiving table, gratified as ghosts and guests help themselves to the plenty. She has cooked with several of them in mind: dairy-free mushroom soup for the lactose-intolerant Bobby; gluten-free kugel for Jean who has celiac disease; a copious medley of vegetables for Jocelyn; and plenty for the omnivores too.

Philip sits on her right and Michael on her left. With Mark on his other side, Michael looks elated and Philip dejected. What has given Caroline such joy now causes heartache for her husband. And how to begin?

Bobby sits next to Norman, who keeps winking at him. "You know what I always think about?" Bobby says. "Those customized reading glasses you used to make me. My eyes needed different magnification, so you used to load up on readers at some flea market, then pop out the one-fifty lenses and put one in the right side of the two-fifty glasses so they were perfect."

Norman smiles.

"When I was sitting by you in the hospital at the end, you were out of it most of the time. But at one point you opened your eyes and said, 'Last chance if you need more reading glasses.'"

"I don't know how you've managed without me," Norman says.

"I use trifocals now."

"Really?"

"I have a question for the group," Bernice says. "When all's said and done, does everyone feel Bill Clinton was a good president? I've always wondered."

"Bill Clinton?" Scott asks, laughing.

"President Clinton. How do you think he did, all and all? Has history been kind to him?"

"Haven't thought of him in ages. Why bring him up in particular?"

"Do you live overseas, Blanche?" Mark asks. Just like Michael, Mark enjoys a game.

"You could say that."

Spencer laughs too. He is seated next to Philip but smiling at Michael. "Mr. Clinton was mostly good, I would say. He had his issues, of course."

"Big issues, but the consummate politician," Philip says.

"You're a lawyer, I'm told?" Michael asks.

Philip nods.

"Where's your office?"

"We recently moved to fifty-six and sixth. We used to be at thirty-third and eighth."

"By the Garden? Fantastic. So, you like sports? I used to live at the Garden."

"Well, I'm at my own small firm now."

"And having problems with a case, I understand."

Philip glares at Caroline. *Why would she share that information?*

"I didn't say anything. He's inside my mind somehow," she says.

"Only when we're in close proximity," Michael says. "It's a power I've never had before."

"Good one," Scott says.

"Originally, my dad was at the World Trade Center," Mark says. "He was there on 9/11."

Michael grimaces upon hearing Mark call Philip *dad*. Caroline feels she should have prepared him for that.

"9/11?" Norman asks.

"The emergency number, Man-nay," Bernice says.

"When the planes flew into the Twin Towers," Jocelyn says. "If our dad hadn't dropped us at school that morning, he would have been up in his office on the eighty-fifth floor."

"Tell them what happened, Dad," Mark says.

Michael grimaces, again.

"Not now," Philip says.

"Come on! Please," Jocelyn says.

Maybe because he can tell how much his kids' attentions disturb Michael, Philip obliges.

"Well, like Julie—I mean Jocelyn—says, I usually went in early, but there was a school-board election that day, so I voted, then dropped the kids off. By the time I came up from the subway into the concourse of my building, all these policemen were ushering us to the doors. They were screaming that we should clear out. I had no idea what was happening. Someone said a plane hit our tower, and I assumed it was a Cessna or something along those lines. Then I went outside." Philip takes a deep breath.

"He saw some terrible things," Caroline says.

Philip motions to her to hold up. "It was total mayhem. I started walking north and was lucky to get Caroline on a pay phone before all the circuits jammed."

"I was dying as you might imagine," Caroline says. "A giant passenger plane had crashed into the building just above his floor. I knew it was the North Tower. And when he called me, we didn't know how many other planes had been hijacked. It was like *War of the Worlds*. Just before he reached me, the second plane struck the South Tower. I told him he had to get out of there, start running north."

"Sounds dreadful," Norman says.

"My goodness!" Bernice says. "How many people were killed?"

"Three thousand!" Scott says.

Bernice shudders.

"My God, how long are we going to play at this? Where've you been hiding, Blanche, under a rock?" Scott asks.

"It's not like they have newspapers in heaven," Caroline says.

"Good one, Caroline," Scott says.

"Anyone from your office?" Michael asks Philip.

"Remarkably, the handful of people already in my office made it down. We were in the first tower, which took longer to fall, but some of them had harrowing stories. It was so dark and smoky, a lot of people on many floors couldn't find the stairs." He looks down. "Two women from our firm died. One had a birthday that day, so the thinking was they'd gone out to breakfast to celebrate and must have been heading up in the elevator when the plane hit."

"The elevators burst into flame," Mark explains. "A minute more and you would have been in the elevator, right Dad?"

"It wasn't your time, Philip," Bernice says. "That's why you were saved."

"I don't know about that," says Jean.

Caroline's voice rises. "I don't believe in that kind of thinking either. I've told them!"

"You go at the right time and it's not scary like we all imagine. It makes sense. It's part of some plan," Bernice says.

"Dear," Norman says.

"You know what happened to me?" Jocelyn says. "Mark was lucky. His guidance counselor took him aside and said, 'Your dad's okay, but something terrible happened at the World Trade Center.' My guidance counselor marched up to me and said, 'Something terrible happened at the World Trade Center'—long pause—'but your dad's okay.'"

Jean brings in two more dishes. "I think we should move onto something else," she says.

"A fulsome feast," Spencer says.

"You know, I was just thinking, it's a real trip down memory lane sitting here," Bernice says, glancing around the room.

Jean sits down beside her. "How do you mean?"

"Well, the furniture. This entire dining room set. Even the silverware."

"Was yours?"

"Once upon a time."

Caroline stands. "Something's missing," she says and heads into the kitchen.

◉ ◎ ◎

Norman finds her sitting in a kitchen chair, her head down. "This is so awkward," she says, "everyone together like this, some of them confused."

"That man Scott's the only one who can't seem to grasp what's going on," Norman says. "But ultimately it won't matter."

"Easy for you to say. You'll be leaving."

"I'm sorry."

"Not as sorry as I am," Caroline says. "And while I have the chance with you alone, I want to apologize for screwing things up on my wedding day."

"What do you mean?"

"I didn't take leave of you properly when you walked me down the aisle. I just let go of your arm and rushed to Michael's side. I was only thinking about him, and us, and getting married."

Norman laughs. "I guess we should have actually rehearsed the night before, but it doesn't matter."

"No. I was supposed to kiss you goodbye and *then* move over to him, and of course I should have known that, but I wasn't thinking."

If she hadn't been so preoccupied, she would have been

soaking in her father's love and pride at giving her away and acknowledged him properly. But as was so often true in her younger days, she was already in the next moment, and her mind and body leapt forward to join Michael. "You had the biggest smile on your face the entire time. The happiest bride I've seen," her mom said afterwards about the ceremony. But she had been in the future, a few steps ahead of herself the whole time.

"I know it bothered you, Dad, because you called me out on it at the dinner afterwards."

"I can't imagine that."

"Yes. I think you had been leaning over to kiss me just as I moved away. I'm sure it was embarrassing."

"I honestly don't remember it."

"That's so curious to me because there's even a picture in my wedding album where we're sitting at the table in the banquet hall and you're admonishing me about it."

"Admonishing you? On your wedding day? I can't imagine."

"I'm sure of it. You look very handsome, but a bit peeved."

"How can you be sure? Maybe we were having a lively debate about something else."

Wow. She had thought about this incident so often, especially after her dad had died. She felt so bad for humiliating him in front of so many people on such a special day.

"It's been one of my major life regrets," she says. "That's why it seemed like such a gift that I could bring it up now."

"Trust me, even if what you say did happen, I never thought of it again," Norman says. "Honest to God."

Caroline knows he is telling the truth, or at least his truth. When you have such good will with someone, they forget even your most egregious blunders. Maybe only a dad can do that for you. Or only a dad who has suffered brain damage?

"Well, anyway, for what it's worth so long after the fact, I'm really sorry." She takes his hand. "I've also worried that I didn't tell you enough how much I loved you."

"You did, Caroline. I knew."

"Well, at least *that* makes me feel better," she says.

Norman motions to the ceiling. "You know, there's something I want to ask you. About something you said when we were upstairs. You said I helped you?"

She smiles. "It's something you told me right before the accident. You and Mom were staying at the house with us, and we took Mark for a walk in the park down the street, just the two of us. Remember the park, by the train station?"

"Of course."

"Well, it was a beautiful day, and we were strolling along, and Mark was being his adorable self. Julie must have been napping back at the house, with Mom. Anyway, suddenly, out of nowhere, you said, 'You know, I always thought you'd succeed at whatever career you pursued, but I didn't realize you'd be such a great mom.' The accident happened three days later, and those words were all I had left. They carried me."

A giant clap of thunder causes Caroline to grasp the tabletop. She's always hearing loud noises—tractor trailers, clanking wagons, ride-on mowers. But this is close by.

"Look at that wind," Norman says. "Look at those branches sway."

A forceful rain ensues, and Caroline turns to her father. "You always loved a good storm."

He pats her shoulder, tears trickling. "I've missed you more than anything."

Norman is her real father. She takes his hand. "Dad."

CHAPTER TEN

Friends will step up when you need them.
—fortune cookie

Stuffed to the gills—an expression Bernice keeps repeating—the group retires to the living room. Philip loves this room above all because it holds so many people, easily accommodating the nine of them now. The crescent-shaped couches hold three each and have been distanced to fit extra chairs at both ends. It's like sitting around a campfire.

At the moment, it's just like a campfire since Mark has constructed a lively blaze in the fireplace.

Only eight of them are in the room, Philip notices; Michael, the spy, has disappeared. *Sneaky and nosy, that one.* Earlier, Philip caught him foraging through the desk drawers in his study.

"Are you for real?" Philip had chided.

"Clever," Michael replied. "I have unfinished business."

"Not with me," Philip had countered.

He suspects he's dreaming. In his dream, Philip sees how Caroline dotes on her former—much younger and otherworldly—husband, but he also feels her affection and fervent reliance on him. It was his hand she took under the tablecloth during dinner. Twice. She has shown him plenty of photos from her past, photos she keeps squirreled away, and they never bothered him because Michael was dead. Gone. And he, Philip, is the one who helped her recover, if not fully move on. She has always relied on him. Once she called him her savior.

"Did you have an accident?" Bernice asks Jocelyn.

"Uh, no. Why would you think that?"

Bernice points to the shaved side of her granddaughter's head. "Thought maybe stitches?"

"You hate it, don't you?"

"Doesn't bother me," Bernice says. "In fact, you remind me of me. You've got flair."

"I do love you're rockin' the polka dots with the desert boots."

Bernice picks up her wineglass and tilts it to down the last few drops. "Would you know if there's any sweet wine floating about?"

"You're a real character, you know that?" Jocelyn says.

"Takes one to know one," Bernice says, then turns her attentions to Spencer. "Forgive me for saying this, Spencer, dear, but you've really aged."

"Only on the outside, my dear. Opposite of you, I guess. Michael tells us you've aged as well, but solely in here." He taps his brain. "That's worse, no?"

"I'm holding my own. Considering. No aches and pains— just pooped. *Old rocking chair's gonna get me.*"

"*Stormy weather,*" Norman intones in a deep bass.

"*Since my gal and I ain't together,*" Spencer adds. A tenor.

Michael returns to the room, squeezing in on a couch beside his father, but only after straightening two of the paintings on the walls. Philip stands, exhales, and walks to the far side of the room to join Scott, who is gazing out the sliding doors onto the back patio.

"A helluva lot of wood you've got there," Scott says. "Is this your answer to buying a generator?" He laughs.

"Maybe. I guess I should deal with it. Or have a bonfire. But Mark's the only one who builds fires around here, when he's here." He makes a mental note to call the tree service, which Caroline picked for its name—*All of the Above*. He likes the name too, and its emphatic slogan. *When price is important and quality imperative.* The company's experts can evaluate and trim their towering oaks and spruces and at the same time haul away the huge piles he's assembled.

The moss on the roof also needs to be dealt with; greenish-gray clumps are encroaching. And the cracked windows. They're not obvious—one in the basement and one on the glass-enclosed porch—but still. Philip gave up his bachelor apartment in the second year of his relationship with Caroline to move into this fine, old house.

Over the years, they have made many improvements, changing out the jalousies for solid windows on the porch and installing heating, upgrading the bathrooms and kitchen, refurbishing the back patio and front walk. He's especially proud of the swing set. At a time when vinyl playground sets were in vogue, all of them featuring the same five-foot slide and four-foot climbing wall, Philip installed an old-fashioned swing set with tall black iron posts and durable turquoise belt seats. The kids' friends loved it because if you pumped vigorously enough, you could swing very high, and because these were different swings than in those ubiquitous playground sets. They are identical to the swings in his family's backyard when he was young.

They have also put in central air, as well as the sliding doors he stands before now.

But as with human beings—though not ghosts apparently—these things, except arguably the swings, have worn over time, and Caroline, generally proactive, has looked the other way, deeming upkeep his responsibility while she maintains the innards of the house.

Growing up, Philip's father had let things go too, alternately calling neglected repairs badges of honor or battle scars. Philip prefers to see wear and tear as rings on their family tree. But the simple truth—money's been tight.

"How's work?" Scott asks, seeming to read his thoughts.

"Fine. Why do you ask?"

"Why wouldn't I ask?"

"Point taken. Sorry. Honestly, right now a few things are giving me fits."

"You're different than I expected," Philip overhears Mark tell Michael. They are looking at the photos on a round glass table. Jocelyn stands a few feet behind Mark.

"How so?" Scott asks Philip.

"Shh," Philip says, trying to hear his son.

"How so?" Michael asks.

"I don't know," Mark says, hesitating. "I don't know what I expected. You're so young, and not exactly my mom's type, at least based on Dad."

Philip smiles.

Michael smiles too. "He's a bit of a stiff."

"I remember when my dad came into my life," Mark says. "'Meet your new father,' Mom said to me and Julie." He looks back at his sister. "She was Julie then. I remember it clearly. But I can't remember you, except for some very hazy images."

"Would have helped if she'd kept our photos out," Michael says. "Well, one thing you should know is, I'm much older than I look. But at the risk of sounding like your nana, I should mention I was quite athletic in my time. You would have been great at sports too, I bet. You have the genes. One of the last things you and I did together was a fun run. Does Brookside still sponsor that 5K, the Turkey Trot? You and I did the mile-long run for kids—they always did that first—and you jogged beside me the entire time. You were game. Took us maybe fifteen minutes, but you had impressive stamina for a four-year-old."

Mark laughs. "That might be the last mile I've ever run without stopping."

"He's a super-fast skater," Jocelyn says.

"I've heard," Michael says, his eyes locked on Mark.

"Did you used to tuck me into bed with a football?" Mark asks. "I feel like I remember that."

"That would be me. And sometimes with my old baseball mitt," Michael says.

Philip is glad Mark can't remember the fun run. Caroline and he did endless activities with the kids throughout their childhood: museums, young-audience concerts, arboretums, aquarium touch tanks, too many visits to The Wild West and Storybook Land. Numerous family trips as well. But Mark and Jocelyn seem to have amnesia about everything before they were fifteen or so. Mark does have a love of travel, though, so these trips and excursions must have made an impression on some level.

"I wish I could remember you," Jocelyn says, moving closer to Mark and Michael.

"You were a newborn," Michael says, his eyes now locked on the photos.

"I was like six months old when you died."

"True. That's still very young."

The man is unable to look at his own daughter. *This Thanksgiving sucks*, Philip thinks, but then he sees Mark smiling at him and he feels so grateful for his son, who hugs him at length whenever he stops by these days.

"Should we check out who's playing now?" Michael asks Mark.

"Can't do that," Mark says. "Mom has a rule—no TV during Thanksgiving."

"She always was a hard-ass about things like that. Good thing I don't have any bets on the games."

An eruption comes from over by the fireplace where Bernice has been bending Bobby's ear for way too long. But they're laughing, some inside joke. The two of them share a scatological sense of humor, according to Caroline. Fortunately, she didn't inherit it.

Philip takes Jocelyn aside. "Didn't that hurt, getting tattooed on your neck?"

"It was pretty painful. But just for a day or two. It doesn't hurt now."

"I hope not."

"I have an idea for the group," Mark says. "But we all need to sit down and close in. Let's go around and tell one of our oldest, or happiest, memories."

The group returns to the chairs and couches.

"They're awfully strange," Philip hears Bobby tell Caroline.

"They were always strange when you think about it," she says.

"That's all you have to say?"

"When you think about it, everyone's strange, right?"

"Thanks," Bobby says. "Very illuminating."

Because of the rain, Scott brings Jupiter back in and the dog nestles at the base of Bernice and Norman's legs, zealously licking at the hole in the toe of Bernice's desert boot.

Jocelyn studies the dog at her ablutions before looking up. "An icebreaker, right, Mark? Like we did in school?"

"I've got a memory," Norman says. "I once worked with a man who had four sons. Two were born on Tax Day, April fifteenth, and another on June fifteenth, and the fourth on September fifteenth. All days when you pay taxes."

"That's weird," Jocelyn says.

"I've got a better one," Bernice says, literally lighting up. "When I was young, my father had an uncle. Uncle Gedalia, we called him, although I don't think that was his real name."

"It's a real name. It's from the Bible," Spencer says. "It means—"

"It's not important," Bernice huffs. "Anyway, this Uncle Gedalia had a huge house in New Jersey, which seemed like another country to me, so far from Brooklyn. Of all my father's relatives, he was the only one with enough space to entertain a huge family of immigrants, and they gathered every month. They called it the Cousins Club, but it wasn't just eating and schmoozing. They had a business meeting to discuss if any family members needed help, and they also made donations to charities from dues they paid. It was mainly for adult family, but one time when I was still a kid, they took me along. I was maybe all of twelve, and everyone fussed over me. 'You're so ugly!' one would say, or 'Yes, isn't she hideous?'—which I soon learned was the highest compliment in Jewish family circles. That was their sense of humor because they didn't want me to get a swelled head. Anyway, there was so much love and generosity toward others in that room. It was really something."

Philip glares at Michael. At first, Michael looks perturbed, but his expression softens as his mother-in-law rambles on. He seems enthralled by her.

The group tells Bernice how wonderful the Cousins Club sounds.

"As is this gathering," she says, gesturing to them all. "*We gather together to ask the Lord's blessing.*"

"She sings!" Michael says. He points to the sliding doors. "Wind's kicking up."

Caroline glances at Philip. "I have an old memory," she says. "From when I was in graduate school. Michael and I were engaged, but living apart, and he flew out to Iowa for the week and attended one of my writing workshops with me. It happened to be my birthday and coincidentally the class was critiquing three chapters from the novel I was working on, my first novel."

"*Capillary Fragility*," Jocelyn says.

Caroline nods. "I still like that title even if it didn't go anywhere. This was the first time the group discussed my work—we took turns submitting material—and to my surprise it was a big hit. Everyone was saying really nice things. They even quoted bits they particularly liked."

"They probably thought you were cute," Jocelyn says.

"I was several years older than most of them, so I don't think it was that."

"Did they know it was your birthday?"

"I don't think they did, Jocelyn. I know it's hard for you to believe, but I think they genuinely liked my work and were very complimentary." She turns to Michael, "And to have you there to witness it all."

He is quiet.

"Remember?"

"You know, I remember coming to visit you—I came out several times while you were there, didn't I? But I don't recall going to one of your workshops."

"Seriously? You seriously don't remember this? Even the professor praised me."

"Are you sure I was there?"

"There are lots of pictures of us in Iowa."

"But none at the actual workshop, right?"

"It was 1988. It's not like I would've brought a camera to the workshop. It's not like now when I could click a quick one with my cell phone."

Michael's face lights up. "Your *Apple* cell phone."

Philip has heard about this workshop many times before. It is indisputably one of the highlights of Caroline's life. "I couldn't have written a more perfect scene," she likes to say about it.

She was in her early thirties and Michael had encouraged her to go to Iowa in the first place. She had applied a year earlier, before she met him, but was hesitant about leaving him unless they were engaged. She told him that one night when they were lying in bed, so he proposed right then and there and that was that.

Michael shakes his head. "I'm sorry. I wish I remembered."

What a schmuck, Philip thinks. *Why can't he just say he was proud of her?*

The room is silent until a branch splits from a tree and hits the ground with a *thwack*.

"You're an asshole," Jean says to Michael.

"Excuse me?" Michael says.

"I think I heard the dessert gong," Caroline says. She turns to Philip, fighting back tears. "Honey, can you help me?" she says with extra emphasis on the word *honey*. "Talk amongst yourselves," she tells the others, her voice cracking.

"It's whipping and swirling, but warming up too," weatherman Michael remarks.

◉ ◉ ◉

Vanilla cupcakes with fudge icing. Autumn-colored macaroons. Powdered donut holes. Mini Key Lime cheesecakes. Berry cobbler with crumble topping. All homemade. And something Caroline has dubbed an upside-down rice pudding surprise. She likes to try something new every Thanksgiving.

"It's bad enough that my mom and dad disagree with me about things that happened, important things, but for him not to remember that workshop at all? I wish *you* could have been there," she says. "Definitely the writing highlight of my life."

"Despite a lustrous career . . . illustrious career?"

"Either works—in my division, of course." She gives him a kiss. "You would have remembered."

"Don't let him get to you. Don't give it a second thought,"

Philip says. "His head has been up in the clouds for who knows how long. Still, this visit is a miracle, and it's obvious why they came now. You've been obsessed with them, Caroline. All that time in the attic. You were calling them. You made this happen."

The last several years have been good ones, perhaps their best. They've continued to have concerns about the kids, but probably no more than most parents, and Caroline has been happy by and large. But ever since she began her reclamation project in the attic, she has been consumed with thoughts of death and her lost family members. She had, indeed, brought this visit on.

"I'm not sure what I wanted from them after all," she says. "I've always been curious what he'd be like when he got older, but he's the same. You always cared much more about my writing, even though he was a writer."

"Maybe that's why."

"I guess you don't mature in heaven," Caroline says.

"Which makes sense since you stop having experiences."

"We shared so much history, but he doesn't even remember."

"You know, the one who surprises me is your mother," Philip says. "You've never painted her in the best light, but she's a sweet old lady."

"I can see that now."

"And quite attractive."

"That, she always was."

They work alongside each other in silence, removing the desserts from their wrappings and arranging them on serving plates that Caroline has lined with lacy doilies. Philip bumps his wife in the hip and she bumps him back. He kisses the side of her beautiful head.

"As bizarre as all this is, it has to be a huge relief to you," Philip said. "You were positive there was no afterlife."

"It's how I was raised. They never talked about heaven in

Sunday school, just how we live on through those we leave behind, who celebrate your memory, but essentially—"

"You're gone. Kaput."

"Right. I mean, I've sometimes wondered if there was something else, if somehow our particles being out in the universe were part of some cosmic spiritual energy. This is much cooler than that."

"It's kind of goofy, the way they describe it," he says.

"But an afterlife nonetheless. I mean, I never minded missing out on Christmas, not having Santa Claus or the Easter Bunny, but the finality of death did prey on me. But here we are. I know in your religion you have all that Pearly Gates stuff, and we've never really talked about this, but did you think you were going to heaven?"

"At my Sunday school, that's all they talked about, 'Be good or you won't go to heaven. Be good or you'll go to hell.' I never gave it that much thought, but I definitely believed we continue on in some way, our souls or spirits, if you want to call it that."

"Not just in the memories of your loved ones?" she asks.

"No, more than that." He takes a bite of a donut hole. "Mmm, so good, honey. I just hope that when they get to the real heaven, there's more to it than where they are now."

◉ ◉ ◉

As they walk toward the living room with large trays, they hear another loud thud from upstairs. Way upstairs. Michael back in the attic. They raise their eyebrows.

"What was that?" Mark says, joining them in the hall.

"Nothing. It's nothing. Don't worry about it," Philip says.

"I bet it's the ladder I was using in the attic. It must have fallen over," Caroline says. She never stops writing.

"Dad, can I ask you something?"

Caroline leaves them together.

"You doing okay?" Mark asks. "I mean, this has to be the most bizarre for you."

"It's certainly strange, but fantastic in a way too, don't you think?"

"I hardly remember them. They're barely familiar," Mark says. "But as long as you're all right with it." He takes the heavy tray from Philip and carries it into the living room.

Mark spent three semesters abroad in college, during which he did much more traveling than coursework. He has been to six continents, jumped out of airplanes, and hiked in the ice-covered Andes. Somewhere along the way, he learned to tune in.

The desserts are displayed on a long card table prepared for this moment. "Wait, wait," Caroline says, jogging to the dining room to retrieve her centerpiece, which she sets on the coffee table, finally cleared of appetizers. Every year she makes a centerpiece, but this time she's outdone herself—an homage to things past with tiny toys, baby socks, tattered baseball cards and paperback pages, dingy old rubber bands and two outsized, chunky candles in the middle.

Everyone makes a fuss when she lights the candles. The total effect is kooky, but dazzlingly bright, as is Caroline's face.

"A Viennese table," Bobby says.

"I remember those!" Norman says.

"You dyed the macaroons?" Bernice asks.

Once they've helped themselves to desserts and are gathered around the fire again, Bobby claps his hands. "If we can crawl out of our sugar stupor, I would like to get back to the present," he says. "I know my sister, who can be very bossy, asked us to hold our questions, but I think it's time. How is it that the three of you came together?"

"We're always together," Norman says.

"It's true," Caroline says.

"But why the three of you? Why isn't Michael with his mother, Isabel, for example?"

"Because you need to form a trio when you die. It's one of heaven's rules," Caroline explains. "Crazy as it sounds."

Bobby shoots her a look. He wants to hear from the ghosts.

"We went together," Norman says, then pauses. "Well, basically."

"And why'd you take so long to visit? And why now?" Bobby asks. "And why just Caroline?"

"Not just Caroline," Bernice mumbles, now swigging a thick Mosel.

"So this *isn't* your first visit," Caroline says. "I knew it, even though Michael kept insisting it was."

"No, no, all I meant is we're visiting lots of you right now, aren't we?" Bernice says.

"Nice recovery, Mom."

"You're really bald, Dad," Michael says to Spencer. "I didn't have a chance to go bald."

"And you're complaining about this?" Spencer counters.

"Still picking up women on the computer, Spence?" Norman asks.

"Now that's a rabbit hole if ever there was one. No one's as she seems."

"Aha, caught you, Dad. How would you know Spencer's dating? More proof you've come before," Caroline says. "You went to see Spencer first, right Dad? How else would you even know about online dating? Plus, Michael knew all these details about Isabel's death."

"We didn't lie to you, darling," Norman tells his daughter.

"No, not you. Michael! And then he blew his cover."

"Michael wanted to tell you we saw Spencer first," Bernice says. "He was trying to, up in the attic. That's what he was going on about with his very roundabout blather about secrets

and surprises." She pauses. "It was hard for him to tell you—
you understand that. Spencer is his father, after all. But in any
event, we only saw Spencer recently. We've only been able to
make visits recently."

"But why would you see Spencer first, Mom? No offense,
Spencer. Michael was *my* husband, and you are *my* parents.
You're only related to Spencer because of me. I'm related
to all three of you, and you are bound together . . . or
were."

"What am I, chopped liver?" Bobby says. "They're my
parents too."

"Don't listen to them," Spencer says. "I hesitate to call your
parents liars, but they're deceiving you here. There were no
earlier visitations. No one came to see me."

"We did," Norman and Bernice say together.

"Hah. No way. I would not forget something like this."

"That's the thing, you'll all forget," Norman says. "It's
another one of the rules. We can come, we can talk—and thanks
to Michael, this time we can eat and make merry."

"And you are thinking better, dear," Bernice says.

"That's true, I'm thinking much better. But once we're gone,
you'll all forget. That's how it works."

"Some feelings may linger," Michael says. "Things you can't
put your finger on."

"Good feelings, we hope," Norman adds.

Everyone is quiet for a time before Spencer speaks. "Wait
a minute. Was it in the spring that you visited me—last April?"

The ghosts nod.

His face flushes as he looks from one to another in the room.
"You know, I think I believe them. I was feeling as low as I'd ever
been that time, around the anniversary of Isabel's death. It was
a glorious spring, her favorite time of year. I was subsisting—
doing anything at all required a colossal effort. That's when I

quit my firm. And then, in an instant, my melancholia was gone, and I felt happy, very happy. So, it was this. This explains it."

"Maybe it was leaving your job," Jocelyn offers. "I love quitting jobs."

Spencer smiles but shakes his head. "I don't think so, dear. It wasn't any one thing. I remember being unable to pinpoint what changed, and so completely. It was inexplicable." He turns to Norman. "Have you seen Isabel up there?"

"We haven't come across her yet," Norman says. "She'll have to be there longer before we can see her, and we have to be there longer before we can connect with older relatives and friends long dead. But, hey, we have plenty of time for it all. There's nothing but time. It's a different continuum."

"I've always believed in heaven or some special place after we die, and I believed in it even more watching Isabel at the end. She was so still, her eyes open, but distant, her breaths growing more and more shallow, and then a look of tranquility and amazement, bliss really, passed over her. Suddenly, she looked much younger, as if her wrinkles disappeared, and she seemed so happy, like she saw something wondrous. And then I saw she had stopped breathing, and I don't know what she saw at the very end, or where she went, but I hope I'm going there too."

The room is silent until Jean finally speaks.

"So, you're saying that the people we've loved and lost—maybe even those who died long ago—are responsible for the times we feel unaccountably happy?"

Norman nods.

"That's amazing," Jean says. "I think my mom has visited me then, maybe lots of times. In fact, I'm sure of it. She died when I was thirteen, and my dad married my evil stepmother less than a year later. But this is different than you're saying because I think she was there for me almost immediately, helping me get through it. Sometimes I thought she'd inhabited the body of this squirrel that was always on my windowsill. Can you sometimes take the shape of animals?"

"Not so sure about that," Norman says.

"Sometimes she gives me signs."

"Like what?" Jocelyn asks.

"Oh, little things I can't otherwise explain. Like her photo will suddenly fall off the bookshelf even though the windows are closed. Like she's trying to tell me something."

"I think I've seen my parents too," Philip says. He can't remember anything specific, but he now believes they are responsible—somehow—for a few great decisions he's made, or when things went right. Or when he felt right, times of unaccountable lightness and joy when he's felt so lucky. No doubt that followed their visits.

"I think my mother helped me realize Scott was the one," Jean says. "And I know she was there when Jeff was born. We had a long conversation. It's funny. I thought these were dreams."

"It's frustrating that the visit's so short," Bobby says. "It would be nice to have more than an evening."

"I know. It's thrilling at first, but then you learn they'll be leaving and it's a killer," Caroline says.

"You won't remember," Norman says.

"We'll just feel better," Spencer says. "I guess it's likely I've had visits by others as well?"

"I would think so," Bernice says.

"Not me. I'm sure you're my first," Mark says.

"There will be more in the future."

"So, we won't remember once you're gone, but you'll remember everything?" Mark asks.

"Yes, it's how we get up to date. We learn so much from these visits," Michael says.

"Seems unfair," Scott says.

"You'll all have this advantage one day."

Scott chortles.

"And we'll simply be deliriously happy?" asks Jocelyn.

"Delirious may be overstating it," Michael says.

Philip watches his wife, who is uncharacteristically quiet. But Caroline looks relaxed, soaking in all that's said, or perhaps away in her own little world. He had noticed that same expression on Norman, pleasantly lost in the sauce just as Caroline is wont to be. *The apple didn't fall far from that tree*, he had thought, and he'd asked Norman what she was like as a child.

"To her, everything was the best," her father had said, "the best movie, the best book, the best teacher, the best life. She was enamored with the world."

Philip heads to the kitchen for something to write on. While his wife is inclined to leave notepads and pens about, she has tidied up for today's gathering, forcing him to resort to one of her private drawers, this one in the base of the farmhouse-style cupboard in the breakfast nook. "Forgive me, honey," he mumbles, pulling it out.

The writing supplies are buried under storage bags of hard candies, Twizzlers, Hot Tamales, and chocolates. There is also her gratitude journal. He opts for a tablet that says *From the brain of Caroline Crane* in a stylish font at the top of each page, a gift left over from when Jules took print shop. He sits at the small desk where Caroline composes her innumerable lists, the bottom of its surface jammed against his thighs as he writes:

Caroline's mom, dad, and Michael visited us at
Thanksgiving. They are bound together in heaven.
They saw Spencer first, back in April. They say we

won't remember their visits, just feel inexplicably
happy once they're gone!!!

He never uses exclamation points!

He folds the piece of paper in half, and in half again, and one more time. Then he tucks it deep into his back pocket.

CHAPTER ELEVEN

The answer you seek is in an envelope.
—fortune cookie

Jean, Scott, and Spencer leave after dessert, as is customary following a huge meal, but Bobby remains with the group in the living room.

"I've been telling . . . him," Mark says. He turns to Michael. "I'm sorry, I can't call you Dad too. It's too weird." He addresses the rest of them. "I've been telling him about my plans for South America."

"Which I fully endorse," Michael says. "I mean, as Mark himself puts it, 'if not now, when?' When you're young, you can afford to take risks, make mistakes, be adventurous, heed only your own desires." He pauses. "Because who knows when that opportunity could be revoked."

"Michael!" Caroline exclaims, aghast that he is quoting from that ominous letter Mark sent home his freshman year, although the line doesn't seem to have registered with her son.

"Who knows, maybe do something illegal," Michael continues.

"That's a terrible idea," Caroline says. *What can he even be thinking of?*

"Spoken like someone who hasn't raised kids," Bobby says.

"I do get your point, within reason, Michael," Caroline says.

"But we don't want Mark making a lot of costly mistakes or doing things he'll regret."

"Mom."

Bobby stands. "I have to go—sorry." He hugs his sister, niece, and nephew, and shakes hands with Philip and Michael. Then he hugs Bernice and Norman for an extra-long time.

"Keep it real, bro," Michael says, then to the others, "be right back."

"He's an antsy guy," Bernice says once Michael is out of earshot. "But well-meaning on the whole, we've learned."

"I guess. Hey, don't forget to take the food for Debbie," Caroline calls after Bobby. "It's right there by the door. Tell her we missed her tonight. And Jason."

⊙ ⊙ ⊙

Michael's resounding, maniacal laugh, followed by objects tossed about and a tremendous clattering, summons Caroline and Philip to the attic. That laugh was almost always accompanied by stomping and slamming doors, Caroline recalls.

They climb the fold-down stairs to find him sitting amidst the rubble, the entire contents of four tall columns of toppled boxes. But instead of looking angry, he looks self-satisfied.

Whatever. Caroline kneels to pick up a bunch of letters and spoils from her boxes that are now commingled with everyone else's. "What a dump!" she says.

"Sorry about this," her first hubby replies. "But I've never seen so many photos and letters."

With the passage of time, she has thought she could whittle down her massive collections. But each snapshot she scrutinizes captures something unique about its subject, something slightly different and special, a smile that curls up at one end and a smile that's fuller and dead on. Although similar, no two photos are exactly alike so she has kept them all.

The letters are about things that matter—lovers, insights, difficulties, joys. She can no longer remember some of the correspondents, but when she can bring herself to delve into them, the pages provide intimacy and support, the voice and revelations of an individual, just as our letters to others help us discover what we are thinking at any given time. Caroline has made copies of some of her best ones before sending.

As emailing and texting have taken over, meaningful correspondence has fallen away. When the internet was new, she used to exchange long, letter-like emails with friends. But over time these have gotten shorter, and now virtually disappeared, replaced by strings of texts, which Caroline can't stand.

It's a pity, she thinks, because letters can surprise us, reminding us of things we've long forgotten or which we never gave their due. Among her stashes, she recently found an effusive card from her mom, written when Caroline was in college. She had come home to visit and left an assortment of her recent writings with Bernice:

> *I want to say a few things, but I hesitate because I can hear you making the judgment that it is natural for me to feel as I do because I am, after all, your mother. But honestly, Caroline, I am also a human being with some education behind me. You, my wonderful daughter, have it. It has been a long time since I laughed out loud and you got me there, several times. Your paper "Looking Out" is priceless. The interview with Charles is a masterpiece of comic understatement.*
>
> *And then some of the essays. I felt glimpses of the beginning of a totally original literary style beginning [sic] to emerge.*

She had been astonished to find Bernice so full of praise. Why had she forgotten this? Perhaps our memories of some people are unfair. Perhaps we remember some people too kindly and others not kindly enough. *How many times*, Caroline wonders, *have I not given my mom enough credit?*

◉ ◉ ◉

"Honey, did you give him permission to poke around up here?" Philip asks now.

"A lot of it is ours," Michael says, his arms spread wide. "And, by the way, *sweetie*, these sheets are filthy." He holds up one of the yellowed bed sheets that had been covering the cartons.

"Give her a break," Philip says. "And stop calling her sweetie."

Michael had always gotten after her about stuff, tidy to a fault. Their two modest incomes had allowed for a professional house cleaning once a month, and in-between he was the one who stayed after things, wiping down surfaces, changing their sheets every week. He was fussy. He would only use Dove soap and carried a bar in a baggie in his toiletry bag for traveling. Towels had to be just the right texture for maximum absorption. Michael complained so often of stinky smells that she called him *The Nose*. Her propensity to build piles had bothered him even then.

In contrast, Philip is neat and hygienic, but tends to wear the same clothes every weekend until she tosses them in the wash. At some point in the past five years, he started wearing eyeglasses full time, and they are usually dotted with specks of dust. She finds it endearing.

While he is oblivious to the state of their house, Philip pitches in. Agreeable and easygoing best describe him. Theirs is the more traditional marriage, in reality, but she has been happy to take on the washing, cooking, and meal prep. She has earned some money from her writing, which she has always done part time, but Philip has worked hard to be the provider.

He is so much easier than Michael. They seldom fight, and though he's a tough adversary when they do, he does hear her side and can be won over.

Thank God it is Philip she's likely to be tethered to in the hereafter, an eventuality that would be a lock, apparently, if they could orchestrate dying simultaneously.

Who will be our third? she wonders.

"Most of the stuff belongs to my parents, Michael. You were too fastidious to be a saver." She looks at Philip. "I guess I did give him permission to look around—implicitly."

Philip turns to Michael. "Well, I want to hear you say it's wrong. And indefensible."

Michael rolls his eyes. "I had unfinished business up here," he says for a second time. "But I'm done now. Want to know some of the stuff I found? Student evaluations from your workshops and literature courses. Impressive, Caroline. You were clearly a hit. Letters I sent to Congressmen right after we got married when I was contemplating switching from journalism to speech writing. I can't believe you held onto those. It didn't work out, but we had a lot of fun in DC that time—remember?"

"No, I don't remember that at all," Caroline says.

"What else did you find?" Philip asks.

"Mark and Julie's schoolwork and doodles, and report cards, most of which are quite mediocre, I must say. I'm really surprised you held onto them."

"I know. Those comments are brutal."

He stoops over to pick up a small plastic pink case. "Birth control pills from the 1800s from the looks of them."

"Whoa, those really go back. Where'd you find them?"

"Stuffed between letters."

"I used to hide them from my mom. She liked to snoop."

"The letters are moving. I never knew Bobby had so many girlfriends or had his heart broken so often. Didn't think he had it in him. And your philosophy professor was obviously in love with you."

"You had no right to read those. Would you have done that if you were alive?"

"Probably not."

"Enough," Philip says. "We need to go downstairs."

Michael laughs, but his color is fading, and he is starting to look translucent again. "By the way, Caroline, what's with all the fortunes? How often do you eat Chinese food?"

"You know I love fortunes. Although I have to say they've really gone downhill over the years."

"How so?"

"They're too general now. They used to be specific and forecast things. Like, 'Beware of a giant pothole next Tuesday.' I kept them to see if they'd come true. Now they're merely aphorisms, things like 'Lovers in triangle not on square.'"

"Presumably your business isn't with Caroline's stuff," Philip says.

"You presume right, but can't a man be curious?" He waves a stack of photos. "Can I keep these, Caroline, please? I'm not sure I can take them back with me, but I'd like to try. And their baby hair—and little bitsy teeth?" He waves plastic baggies containing these items, which Caroline has labeled. "Can I keep these too?"

"Sure."

"By the way, I think I've made a connection with Mark, but I can't find a way in with Julie."

"Talk to *Jocelyn* like anyone else," she says.

"Okay. Next time. Why does she look like this?"

"She'll get over it."

Caroline presses Michael's side to see if he has ribs. She doesn't feel anything. "You've made me feel better, all of you, but I'm still afraid of dying," she says.

"Really? Still? One of the main reasons for our coming here was to allay your fears, let you know we continue on in the universe. Have we made a little headway at least?"

"Probably not with Caroline," Philip says. "She can't help it. Death and dying are her default mode. She's impossible to reassure."

"That's my Caroline," Michael says.

"That's *my* Caroline," says Philip.

It struck her as very smug, on both of their parts, but could she really argue with what they were saying?

"We go on, Caroline. We persist. We endure," Michael continues. "We're your proof that there's life in the hereafter."

"Of sorts," Caroline says.

"I remember you always fretting about time passing you by. It should delight you to know there's so much more ahead of you, even after you die. And by the way, lots of Jewish thought considers the possibility of heaven. You were wrong to think it's so absolute about the end of life."

"That's what I was taught."

"Things proceed slowly—very slowly—but it's relaxing and not unenjoyable. And at last, after nineteen years, we're starting to ramp up our experiences, and they will keep getting richer. But our time here's nearly up." He stops, clears his throat, twice. "So now, before we go, I believe I'm in a position to help you two. I've learned you're in financial straits."

"Caroline!"

"Aren't we?" she asks Philip.

"Yes, but—"

"I thought so."

Philip's face reddens. "And you shared this with him? I really don't appreciate your sharing this with him."

"I didn't say a thing. I swear."

"Then—"

"He can read my mind, Philip. Literally!"

Philip snorts.

"Imagine how I feel," Caroline says. "So, don't yell at me."

"I'm sorry. I'm just overextended right now, that's all. It's the Brinkman lawsuit. You know all about it, Caroline."

"But you said it was going well?"

"It was until it wasn't. And while we're at it . . . Honey, something else has happened."

"Which is where I believe I come in." Michael removes a sheet of paper from an envelope and hands it to Caroline.

"What's this?" she asks. "Stocks?" She hands the sheet to Philip.

"This is the thing I was looking for," Michael says. "It's a present, for both of you. In January 1996, I invested twenty thousand in Apple stock. And that March I abruptly died."

Philip studies the paper. "Holy crap! This has to be worth a fortune."

"Upwards of two million now," Michael says. "Two-point-four mil, in fact. I checked it out on her computer. I did a Google search, Caroline," he says with pride.

"And you're giving it to us?" she asks.

He shrugs like it's nothing. "Well, you could use it more. It's no good where I come from. You really can't take it with you. I'm not even sure I can take these souvenirs." He clasps the baggies of teeth and hair to his heart. "But I'm gonna try."

"Where did the initial twenty thousand come from? And how come you never told me about it?" Caroline asks.

"Remember the money I inherited from my Grandpa Irwin? We had talked about putting it in a college fund for the kids, but I took a flier. I know it was risky, and I realize now how hard it was for you to pay for Mark's education, which I feel bad about."

Philip winces.

"But how did you expect me to find it?" she asks.

"I didn't. I thought I'd be here. I wasn't expecting to die in a car accident, Caroline. Hang on." From a heap in a corner of the room, he picks up a varnished wooden box. "Remember this? It was in here. I hid it a long time ago and I couldn't remember where. Hence the mess. I went through everything. This was a gift from my mom, for my bar mitzvah. She was so sweet." His initials are engraved on the lid.

"You loved that box," Caroline says.

"It's a magician's box. Look—it has a false bottom." He lifts the lid and removes the bottom to reveal a compartment beneath. He laughs. "A darn good thing you didn't know about this 'cause you probably would have cashed it in long ago, way too early. From what I was reading, Apple did terribly for years while Microsoft and IBM stocks steadily increased. But then Apple had this iPod gadget and some type of portable phone that exploded in popularity. I guess that's the walkie-talkie thingamajiggy you were using before, Caroline? Apple stock has gone berserk."

Caroline gasps. "I just thought it was a pretty box."

"So, my little secret is now my great surprise," Michael says. "Philip, mind if I kiss your lovely wife?" Before Philip can answer, Michael has placed his hands on Caroline's arms and planted a longish kiss on her lips.

"That's enough, you," she says, pushing him away.

"That was only meh," Michael says.

⊙ ⊙ ⊙

With the grandchildren's parents in the attic with Mark's real father, and the grandparents' daughter in the attic with her two husbands, Mark, Jocelyn, Bernice, and Norman sit on the living room couches staring at each other.

"I see you're a fan of my mom's work?" Jocelyn finally says, pointing to the paperbacks at Norman's feet.

He smiles. "Lifelong!"

Bernice leans forward, wiggles to the edge of her seat. "Well, I guess it's high time we got to know each other," she says. "These otherworldly visits aren't just for the living, you know. Imagine how hard it's been for us not knowing what's gone on with you, and to be deprived of indulging you."

"I think I remember helping you in the kitchen. We used to make things, didn't we?" Mark asks. "Didn't you have a lot of animal cookie cutters at your house?"

Bernice smiles. "Goodness, you remember that? Yes, you were my enthusiastic assistant. We made cut-out cookies, and pumpkin bread, and Eggs in a Nest. I'm touched you remember."

"Was Eggs in a Nest the egg in the middle of the bread? I made that all the time with Mom," Jocelyn says, "only she called it Birds in a Bush."

"I'm not surprised. She's a writer. She likes to change things."

"What happened to your shoe?" Jocelyn asks.

Bernice holds out the desert boot with the hole cut out exposing her big toe. She laughs. "It's a new style in the great beyond. Thought you'd like it." She tugs on her polka-dot skirt. "There's something I want to ask you. What's with all the keys?"

Jocelyn jiggles the large, shiny ring of rainbow-colored keys on her belt loop. "They're not all real. Some of them remind me of things I want to focus on, but I'm kind of locked up about."

"Heavy," Mark says, elbowing his sister. "Hey, can I call you Joss?"

"Okay, I guess. I'm not exactly sure what I'm doing," Jocelyn tells Bernice.

"You were such adorable little children," Bernice says. She squeezes Jocelyn's hand. "We didn't know you as well, of course, but you were a beautiful, eensy-weensy baby and we were thrilled you came to us."

"Really?" Jocelyn asks.

"Of course," Bernice says.

"Absolutely!" Norman says. "You must know there were no reservations?"

"When did you learn you were adopted?" Bernice asks.

"Not till I was twelve. According to the research, it should have been earlier."

"What do *you* think?" Norman asks.

"I don't know. But I can tell you, one of the first things people ask when they hear I'm adopted is, 'When did you find out?' They want to know when I was adopted and when I found out about it."

"Why does it matter?" Norman asks. "I'm sure you always felt your parents' unconditional love. They were wild about you, and it's the same today, with your mom, and your new father."

"He's not so new. He's my third father, but the only one I've really known, which is bizarre."

"It's obvious how much he loves you," Bernice says.

Jocelyn sighs. "I know they love me. It's just that, essentially, they lied to me all those years before they told me the true circumstances of my life, who I really was."

"But it never came up, did it?" Mark asks. "And if it never came up, how were they lying to you?"

"It was a lie of omission, Mark, I think Dad would say. It was misleading not to be told because of course I assumed I was their child by birth, and your real sister, although you and Mom always seemed to have more in common and I felt different. But they had all those baby pictures."

"You were only about a week old when your mom found you," Bernice says.

"Right. We don't even know how old I was. And I just think it's unfair that Mark knew the secret all along when I didn't."

"Jules, how many times do I have to say this. I learned right before you did—Joss, I mean."

"I know that's your story, Mark, but I think that's a lie too. I mean, didn't you think it was strange that you never saw Mom pregnant and then I just appeared? You must have seen your friends' mothers pregnant. Didn't you wonder why she didn't get huge, and tired? What about that?"

"I didn't think about it for a second. I was four, Joss—what did I know? A four-year-old boy doesn't think about these things, trust me. All I thought about back then was lawnmowers and garbage trucks. And that toy drill I had. Remember that?"

"Yeah, you loved that. But what about when you got older?"

"The only thing I ever thought was strange was that they brought you home the day before Halloween, but they said you were born on October first."

"So how'd they explain that?"

"They told me you were a preemie and had to stay in the hospital a while."

"Aha, my point! That's an outright lie."

"No, it's true," Norman says. "You were in the hospital a while."

"They didn't want to tell me your story before they told you," Mark said. "How can you blame them for that?"

"I'm sure they had the best intentions," Norman says. "It's

a hard one to navigate. I bet they were waiting until you could fully comprehend."

"When I was a young woman, parents never told children they were adopted," Bernice says. "Maybe that was better."

"I was just happy you were a girl," Mark says.

"Really?" Jocelyn says.

He smiles. "Yup. I wanted a little sister. All my friends had siblings and it seemed to me sisters were easier."

She smiles. Mark thinks she is less touchy than usual. Maybe her time away is working.

"October first was a completely arbitrary date for my birthday."

"A best estimate," Norman says.

"And I can never meet my birth parents. I can't even search for them. That's the other thing people ask, 'Do you know your birth parents?'"

"The police searched long and hard for them, and the Department of Family Services," Bernice says. "But now you could do a 23andMe, Myself, and I test, couldn't you?"

"They can't give you a match unless your parents are also in the database—if they've submitted their DNA too. But how likely is it that my parents are on 23andMe or any of those sites? They don't strike me as very family oriented. I mean, I guess I could try to investigate, but what's the point of trying to find people who have no interest in finding you?"

"But you could learn about your origins."

"This way I can be whoever—whomever," Jocelyn says. "That appeals to me, at least right now."

"I get that," Bernice says. "I'm also a fan of pink, by the way." She touches Jocelyn's braid.

"Nana, how do you know about DNA testing?" Mark asks.

"When we visited Spencer that other time, his cousin had just done one. Apparently, his family line goes back to an ancient king of Scotland who happened to be Shakespeare's big patron!"

"Why am I not surprised," Jocelyn says. "It's strange that Mark and mom are the only blood relatives in our family."

"And Uncle Bobby and Jason. And Nana Bernice and—." Mark turns to Norman, "What did I call you?"

"Norpa," Norman says proudly. "For Norman and Papa."

"Norpa?" Jocelyn says.

"I think I remember that too," Mark says. "Anyway, Joss, you're right. Philip isn't my real dad either. We share that. And if I wanted an axe to grind, I could be mad at Mom for telling me so little about my real father all these years. And hiding all those photos."

Jocelyn shrugs. "Well, you guys don't have to worry about me. All this stuff only bothers me a little. I've adapted to being adopted. I've found plenty of other things to be hung up about. And I'm looking at college applications again. I think I should go back to school."

"That's great," Mark says. "Mom and Dad will be ecstatic."

"Don't say anything. I'm not ready to tell them yet."

Bernice takes Jocelyn's hand again. "I went to college later, too."

"You went to college?"

"Sure, but not till your Uncle Bobby started kindergarten."

"Wow, that's neat. What did you study?"

"I studied nutrition, believe it or not. I didn't finish." Bernice hung her head.

"So, what happens, one day you just wake up dead?" Mark asks. "It's all so neither here nor there."

"We're not allowed to tell," Norman says.

"But, yeah, sort of," Bernice whispers.

"It's pretty cool actually," Norman says.

"Norman!"

"What? I can say that. That doesn't give anything away."

"I have a question for you guys," Mark says. "If you could have chosen, how would you have wanted to die?"

"Older, of course," Bernice says. "It would have been grand to have more time. But this wasn't bad when all's said and done. It was quick and there's something that happens that's quite lovely, which we're not at liberty to disclose."

"It can't be put into words. It's impossible to describe," Norman says.

"I think about death a lot," Mark says. "I have a whole collection of books on the subject. I haven't read them yet, but I plan to one day. I want to be ready, or at least more at peace with it than my mom."

"What do you think about your lives when you look back on them?" Jocelyn asks. "I mean, now that you have all this perspective?"

"We had a wonderful life," Norman says. "We really did. We were very lucky. But it's true that we appreciate it all much more in hindsight. The trick is to do it in real time."

"You know, my mother, your great grandmother, used to tell me, 'You'll see. It's like a dream. One day you're a child and the next you're an old lady.' And you know what?" Bernice looks up and gestures to the ceiling, "You were right, Ma." She leans far forward to take both of her grandchildren's hands. "I wish I'd been less critical . . . and complained less and focused on all the good things. The key is to be positive." She releases their hands and straightens in her chair. "But life can be hard, and sometimes my attitude sucked."

CHAPTER TWELVE

Peace of mind comes piece by piece.
—fortune cookie

She didn't get the chance to tell Bobby that Norman isn't their real father, Caroline realizes—not that it matters since he would have forgotten as soon as he left the house. She too will forget once the ghosts are gone, and she is glad she won't remember the long-held secret her mom had disclosed—that her uncle is her genetic parent.

"If I'm not going to remember anything, why the urgency to tell me Dad's not my real Dad?" she had asked Bernice, who had turned pale, looking puzzled herself.

"Because of those damn DNA tests. You might have done one," she had stammered.

"But couldn't you have left that to chance since I wouldn't have retained the helpful explanation for your needing Uncle Bruce's sperm anyway?"

"Hey, Caroline, I'm almost eighty. Being a little goofy is entirely appropriate in my division. I can't think out all the twists and turns."

She had hugged her mother then. "I'm sorry."

"You'll have been enriched for having seen us," Michael says now in the attic. "In more ways than one," he adds, a not-so-subtle reminder about the stocks.

Philip nods his appreciation with another wince of pain. "Thank you again for that," he says. "It's a huge help."

She will forget everything, but nevertheless be wildly uplifted by their visit, or so the ghosts insist, although the thought of losing them again makes her shudder. It's crazy to think she will lose them again.

Still, she considers her first husband, whom she once regarded as nearly perfect, and is struck by the thought that his departure will be a relief.

Up the attic steps clomp her parents. "How great are those kids!" Norman says at the top, leaning on the railing, breathless.

"Yes, you should be very proud of them, dear," Bernice says to Caroline, then turns to Philip. "You, too."

"I love you, Mom," Caroline says, her eyes brimming with tears.

"We are all better for these visits," Norman says. He and Michael take turns shaking Philip's hand, then Norman takes Caroline into his arms. "Be seeing you, darling," he says.

"Soon, please," she says.

When it's Michael's turn, he envelops her. He has retained his unique smell, but it's faint.

"So, this is it? You're all going?" she asks, finding it hard to breathe.

"Actually, it is you who must go—immediately, I'm afraid. We've pushed our time here to the brink."

"You want *us* to go?"

He releases her. "That's the last rule. We have to leave unwitnessed from the place we first appeared." He motions to the attic steps. "Time to return to earth."

Michael steps back, injecting himself between her parents and becoming imperceptibly attached to them once more. The color drains out of them until they're black and white and all the modifications that formed their transformation are undone.

The ghosts' glassy fingers point to the stairs. "Please!" they say in unison.

The couple descends.

◉ ◉ ◉

The night was anything but clear at eight as Caroline, Philip, Mark, Jocelyn, and Jupiter—in the lead and straining at her leash—trudged up the hill half a mile toward the house at the top of their street where the Simon family lived. The wind churned, causing leaves to swirl around their faces, but it had warmed considerably since their guests had arrived for the holiday supper. They were sweating in their winter gear.

While grabbing his coat, Philip had noticed that a new text from Jessica had come in earlier:

Just saw Ted on the evening news.

He's holding his wife and daughter

hostage at gunpoint. Police have

surrounded their house.

What was he supposed to do with this information? Major compartmentalizing now in order!

Caroline hummed the tune "Stormy Weather."

"It feels like we're going skiing," Jocelyn said.

"But it's balmy out here," Philip said.

"Well, the wind reminds me of when we're skiing. This wind is nuts," she said. "I love skiing. I feel euphoric. That was, like, the best Thanksgiving ever. I don't even know why. Just something about it."

"I agree," Mark said. "Unaccountably great. Mirific."

"Huh?"

"I feel happy. We're all so lucky," Jocelyn said.

"And didn't your mom do a great job with the food?" Philip asked.

"Off the charts," Jocelyn said.

"Homeric," Mark said.

Caroline laughed. "Thanks y'all!"

She felt happy too, as if she were in a different place. She felt invincible. Maybe she could drastically reduce the attic clutter once and for all, retaining just a smattering, a few lovely reminders rather than bins full of what felt like chores. Simplify her life.

The Simons were old friends, another nucleus of five if you counted their dog, Sparky, who was the only non-human creature Jupiter would abide. The two families had lived in the neighborhood for more than two decades and each of them had a valued counterpart in the other's unit. For years they had been having five-way playdates, and tonight they had been invited for a nightcap. Beth Simon also liked to start her Thanksgiving celebrations early, so by evening her guests were also gone.

As her family topped the hill, Jocelyn said, "By the way, I'm not going into the whole Jocelyn thing with the Simons. I don't feel like it."

"Jules, you're a gem," Philip said. It was something he had said all the time when she was a little girl, but maybe not for several years. He put his arm around her and she placed her arm on top of his. Her eyes filled.

Caroline hummed.

"*You're* happy," Mark said.

"I really am. How could I not be—having you guys here. And there really was something special about tonight."

◉ ◉ ◉

The Simons' house was toasty; they too had built a fire that night, the embers of which were fading out. The dogs were released into the fenced-in backyard and Richard Simon passed around colorful cordial glasses of Grand Marnier. Mark and Will, the Simons' son, opted for beers, which they took into the basement.

"Anybody want something to eat?" Beth asked.

"Yeah, because we're starving," Philip said.

Beth laughed. "So, who all did you have over today?"

"Oh, just the usual," Caroline said. "My brother Bob, although his wife wasn't feeling well so she took a pass, and he wouldn't tell us what their teenage son was up to. And Spencer, of course, and our friends Jean and Scott. So, a little smaller than usual, although it didn't feel that way."

"It really didn't," Julie said.

"What about Jean and Scott's son? Is it Jeff?" Meredith Simon asked.

"Yeah, but he's in Japan, teaching English."

"Cool."

"Scott's a great guy," Richard said. "He's so jovial."

"That he is," Philip said.

"Okay if Julie and I go up to my room?" Meredith asked her mom as she motioned for Julie to follow her.

"Sure, go ahead," Beth said. She turned to Philip and Caroline. "We were smaller than usual too, which was kind of nice. We did a lot of reminiscing with the kids. They just love that." She laughed.

"For some reason we talked a lot about 9/11," Philip said. "And Caroline's mother's infamous stories."

◉ ◉ ◉

Evidently, back at their home, the last one out hadn't fully closed the front door, didn't realize it hadn't clicked shut but rather blown open, causing the roaring wind to knock over the chunky candles that were burning full tilt in the center of Caroline's homemade wreath.

The candles' flames had ignited the crumpled paperback pages and tattered cardboard baseball cards and origami birds comprised of old letters from Caroline's long-lost pen pals. A fragment of paper with a small flame fell onto the rug, which in turn ignited the chairs and couches, and the books, law journals, and decorative straw baskets in the tall, wooden bookcases. Hot air and smoke spread across the ceiling. Dense smoke and intense heat traveled through the hallway and into the other rooms and up the stairway to the second floor. Within a few minutes, as the heat intensified, objects spontaneously burst into flames.

At the Simons' home, the dogs' incessant barking was the first sign something was amiss. Then came the sirens of the fire trucks. Many fire trucks, very close. Philip's cell phone rang.

"This is Chief Sullivan from Fire Station Three," a deep voice said. "Do you live at Seventeen Tree Swallow Lane?"

"I do," Philip said.

"Is anyone in the house? It's on fire!"

"No, we're up the street," Philip said, running to the Simons' front door and opening it wide. "We'll be right there." A blast of wind smacked him in the face and heavy fire smells overwhelmed him.

Caroline followed him outside, mumbling something about leaving the kids there.

The burning smells intensified as they hurried down the hill, and as they got closer, the smells were not just of fire, but of burning rubber, wires, and combustibles. They covered their mouths with their hands.

The flames were everywhere, pulsing through the windows and out the front door. The shutters had been devoured and the yellow and orange blaze now engulfed the ledges and roof. You couldn't see large portions of their house anymore.

"Stay back," the fire chief yelled as the distraught couple approached, rapidly.

"So fast!" Philip said.

Chief Sullivan nodded. "Thank you for not thinking of rescuing anything. It was too far gone when we got here, I'm afraid. High winds are a powerful accelerant. I'm sorry, but I have to ask you to stand behind the barrier now."

A small crowd had gathered behind them on the gentle hill where policemen were setting up a barricade. When they finished, they formed a human wall in front of it to contain the crowd. Several firemen continued to hose the house.

The chief ushered Philip and Caroline behind the barricade. "Any idea how it might have started?" he asked.

They shook their heads no.

"Anything left on the stove? Were you using the fireplace? Candles?"

"Oh my God, the candles—in the wreath," Caroline said.

"But could they consume a whole house this fast?" Philip asked.

"Fires burn much faster these days because everyone has so much synthetic stuff."

"We don't!" Caroline said, although she wasn't sure. Mostly, between Philip's stores of magazines and journals and all her scribblings, it seemed the two of them amassed paper.

A giant gust of wind assaulted their faces. Sparks lit the reddening sky.

"And the wind," the fire chief added. "The front door was wide open. Went right in."

◉ ◉ ◉

In some portions of the house, mushrooms of gray smoke now replaced the flames. The sawhorses had been moved farther back, and like the others in the crowd, Caroline and Philip's only role was that of a spectator.

Philip put his hands into his front pockets and pulled out an envelope. Inside was a thick piece of paper, a certificate for twenty-thousand shares of Apple stock. "What the heck! Honey, where'd this come from?" He handed it to her.

She looked it over. "Beats me. What is it? You know I have a mental block about financial forms."

"It appears to be an investment you own—in Apple stock. Which makes it incredibly valuable."

"I've never seen it before. Why's Michael's name on it too? Where's it from? How'd you get it?"

"I have no idea. It was in my pocket, but I bet it's worth a fortune."

Caroline blanched. "Really?"

"I'm pretty sure. I have this client who's always telling me how he put all his savings in Apple stock. It was an up-and-down ride, but in the last several years it's skyrocketed. His portfolio's worth a fortune."

"Oh my God. Did you find it in the attic?" she asks.

"This is the first time I'm seeing it. You know I'm only in the attic to fetch you. You had to have put this in my pocket, Caroline."

She shook her head. "I didn't—but thank goodness that's where you put it."

Philip patted down his pants and pulled out another paper, this one from a back pocket.

"Wait, there's more," he said, extracting a single sheet that had been folded in half, and in half again and again to form a compact rectangle.

"Are you doing origami now?" Caroline asked with a flicker of a smile.

The sheet was blank, front and back, except for a heading, *From the brain of Caroline Crane*. He showed her. "And why would I be walking around with this?"

◉ ◉ ◉

Mark, Jocelyn, and the Simon family squeezed through the thick crowd, searching for Caroline and Philip. Beth Simon took the sobbing Jocelyn into her arms.

"Thank God we had Jupiter with us," Jocelyn said between gulps of breath.

"Stand back. You must stand back," the fire chief yelled to the gathering in general.

Mark rested his hand on Jocelyn's shoulder.

"It's the only home I've known, Mark. They bought it before I was born. At least you had another one."

"That was an apartment. Mom showed it to me once. We lived there till I was three, but I don't remember it."

"So many trucks," Richard Simon said. He read the names to himself: *heavy rescue, hook and ladder, pumper truck*. "So many different kinds." He didn't know what else to say . . . or do. He felt so sorry for his friends, and so lucky that it wasn't his house.

Caroline and Philip caught up with their group, and when Caroline took Jocelyn into her arms, her daughter broke down.

"*Shh,*" Caroline said. "We'll be okay, all of us." She nestled her chin into the top of Jocelyn's head. "I know you've said you need to be on your own, but you'll always have a home with us wherever we are, you know that?"

"Absolutely, Jocelyn," Philip said. "You too, Mark. Don't worry."

Mark looked very worried, his forehead sweaty. And Philip looked so sad.

"Well, wherever it is, I'm going to visit you more there," Jocelyn said.

"That would be great," Philip said.

"We'd love that," Caroline added.

The fire chief motioned for the couple to join him at the first barrier.

"I'm sorry we couldn't do any more than put this inferno out," he said.

◉ ◉ ◉

Caroline shivered as she looked at the remains of the house and at Philip. He was looking at her, away from the conflagration, his handsome face backlit by the surging flames. His blue eyes were paler than when she first met him, but they were loving and wise, even as observed behind the ever-present specks of dust on his eyeglass lenses.

She could see how devastated he was, and she couldn't fathom why she wasn't more upset.

She took his hand. "All houses hold secrets," she said. "Words we wished we'd said. Words we wished we could take back. Things we weren't told. Things we told others too late. Things we could have done better."

Philip turned to face the house. The large lilac bush was ablaze.

It came back each spring, so aromatic. He loved that bush. He faced Caroline again, closed his eyes. "You lived here for years," he said softly. "What's wrong with you? Why aren't you more upset?"

"I'm trying to stay strong for the kids. I'm sure I'll be a mess later, but I've switched into emergency mode."

"All that stuff, yours—and theirs. You always said you needed it."

She was thinking of the blue lacquered box with Michael's love letters, all those light blue sheets she could never throw out. Well, they were gone now, and she was glad. "Things we hid from others. Things they hid from us. Maybe a box with a false bottom. Have you ever seen one of those?"

"Nope."

"Me neither. I'd like to, though. They always sounded cool to me."

"What made you think of that?" Philip asks.

"I have no idea."

"Well, so many boxes, Caroline. I thought you needed all that stuff to keep the record straight. For your writing. That's what you always said."

"I've come to realize there is no 'straight.' I've had a huge sea change."

All that stuff was more a trap than a treasure—Caroline was certain now. There were so many things we didn't remember, or didn't remember right, and who wanted to maintain a reference library? Our impressions and emotions were what stuck with us no matter what, not the facts—and maybe that was all we needed, not tons of documentation.

"Some memories mean the world to us, but nothing to others. Everyone has a different version of the past, even if you were in the same room. I guess it's neat if you see it that way," she said.

"That's what makes for horse racing," Philip said, almost smiling.

"Right. It's why I'm fascinated by eulogies and toasts. Everyone has their own take. We all mean such different things to others." She squeezed his hand. "It's what makes for characters."

A giant piece of the front wall crashed to the ground and Philip pulled Caroline closer to him.

"I'll count on remembering the past whichever way I can. The rest I'll make up," she said.

The last thing to go was the attic, but now its contours too were swallowed by flames.

"But it seemed like you were starting to pull things together up there," he said.

"You're joking, right? It was total chaos. Tohubohu. And I'm telling you, it doesn't matter. Better to move forward, as you're fond of saying. Aren't you always telling me I need to let go? Voila!"

"I wasn't speaking literally. What about your letters?"

"Hmm." She would miss the letters, and the photos. She would miss them dearly. "You got me there."

"And what about all those notes for your books?"

"Those were a trap for sure."

Her novels had incubated for a long time, during which she made countless notes; for her latest work, she had filled two shoeboxes with them—ideas, possible dialogues, and plot developments. But she rarely referred to them, and when she did, they usually spun her backwards instead of forward. The story and characters had moved beyond them, taking their own twists and turns. Jotting things down advanced the process, but then she had to let the text evolve spontaneously, not insert all the things she had pondered along the way. When she stayed in the here and now of the story, that's when the magic happened.

"I can't work from slips of paper, Philip. I have to trust that the essential things have been internalized. The manuscript itself is safe in Dropbox, thank God."

The intense light from the flames created a halo around her face and Philip thought she never looked more beautiful.

"Too much time lost to sorrow," she said.

He kissed her. "Undying love and lust," he said, her glass-half-full specialist.

"We had some wonderful times there."

"Lots of wonderful times."

"But not nearly enough times when I told you you're the best," Caroline said, kissing him back. Then she said of the house, "It will be all right, you'll see. Like rewriting from scratch. You know how much better things are when you start over."

ACKNOWLEDGMENTS

It is fitting that my novel is set during Thanksgiving because I am very thankful for the many friends and relatives who care about my writing journey.

I would like to thank my mother, Carol Sherman, for the constancy of her love and belief, and my sister, Tami Sherman, a discerning reader who forever helps me with highs and lows. My brothers, Chuck and Jamey Sherman; brothers-in-law, Tom Hitchcock and Tom Rodriguez; nephews, Adam and Eric Rodriguez and Bryan Sherman; and grandson Hayden Hitchcock, all serve as inspiration.

Much appreciation to Publisher John Koehler for graciously shepherding this project, and to Executive Editor Joe Coccaro for his terrific edits and suggestions. And special thanks to Christine Kettner for capturing the spirit of my novel so well in both the design of the interior and her wonderful cover.

Thanks to Helane Russo for an early read and steadfast support, and to Jane Schwartz for her astute edits. Much gratitude to Nancy Gerber and Ina Lancman for their encouragement and perceptive feedback on two drafts, and to Wendy Newman for her keen observations and for suggesting I deepen the novel's major themes.

My children are a wellspring of love and support for which I am extremely grateful. To my daughters-in-law, Maggie Hitchcock and Ali Viterbi, for their insights and enthusiasm. To my son, Peter Hitchcock, for his ongoing help with concerns and perspective, not all restricted to writing. And to my son, Sam Hitchcock, for an invaluable critique and for frequent bolstering to spur me on.

It seems I need a lot of bolstering, which my husband, Christopher Hitchcock, supplies in droves. He is my mainstay, patient and kind. In addition to everything else at which he excels, Chris is a talented editor and plot guru. He makes my writing, and my life, so much richer.

CPSIA information can be obtained
at www.ICGtesting.com
Printed in the USA
JSHW011331071222
34447JS00001B/3